LATER ON

LATER ON

THE MONAGHAN BOMBING MEMORIAL ANTHOLOGY

Compiled and edited by Evelyn Conlon

First published in 2004 by
Brandon
an imprint of Mount Eagle Publications
Dingle, Co. Kerry, Ireland
in association with the Arts Office of Monaghan County Council

2 4 6 8 10 9 7 5 3 1

ISBN 0 86322 325 7 (hardback)
ISBN 0 86322 326 5 (paperback)

Cover design: Anú Design [www.anu-design.ie]
Typesetting by Red Barn Publishing, Skeagh, Skibbereen
Printed in the UK

CONTENTS

ACKNOWLEDGEMENTS

My thanks to the Committee of Monaghan Memorial Art Commission for their support while compiling this book. Particular thanks to Somhairle Mac Congail, arts officer, and the staff of the office; Paudge McKenna; Anthony McDonagh, town clerk and his staff; Billy Moore, former town manager; the staff of Monaghan County Library and Rathmines Public Library; Jenny Haughton and Margaret Urwin of Justice for the Forgotten, Dublin.

Special thanks to relatives of those killed, in particular to Marie Coyle and Eileen McCague, and also to those who called into the Arts Office to talk out their thoughts, and of course to the authors for their patience as the book changed and took shape. This publication was made possible with the assistance of the Arts Office of Monaghan County Council, financially supported by ADM/CPA, an implementing body under the EU Programme for Peace and Reconciliation, Monaghan County Council and Monaghan Town Council.

My thanks to the authors and/or the publishers for permission to use published work. All efforts have been made to contact copyright holders.

Leland Bardwell, *The White Beach*, Salmon Publishing, 1998
Evelyn Conlon, *Skin of Dreams*, Brandon, 2003
Shane Martin, *Stilling the Dance of Time*, Black Lane Books, 2001
Eugene McCabe, *Death and Nightingales*, Secker & Warburg, 1992
Patrick McCabe, *Call Me the Breeze*, Faber and Faber, 2003
Ted McCarthy, *November Wedding and Other Poems*, Lilliput Press, 1998
Aidan Rooney-Céspedes, *Day Release*, Gallery Press, 2000
Pádraig Rooney, *In the Bonsai Garden*, Raven Arts Press, 1988
Peter Woods, *Hard Shoulder*, New Island, 2003
Robert Janz's work can be seen at *www.driftdiary.com*
Information on Justice for the Forgotten can be seen at *www.dublinmonaghanbombings.org*

Permission to publish Patrick Kavanagh's poems was received from the trustees of the estate of the late Katherine B. Kavanagh, through the Jonathan Williams Literary Agency.

Don Mullan allowed me to quote from his interviews published in *The Dublin and Monaghan Bombings*, Wolfhound Press, 2000.

INTRODUCTION

SOMETIMES AN INTRODUCTION to a book teeters nervously and is cautious about raising its head above the parapet, not quite sure what to say. This one is most certainly of that school. From the start of this project, begun when I was convinced by the Monaghan Memorial Committee that it was both desirable and possible, I have been continuously uneasy about this book. Never mind how it would be done, and how the three components would sit together, but also what it actually is.

Let me address first the components. One section was requested from writers born in County Monaghan or long resident there. This included non-fiction as well as fiction and poetry. Another portion was given to the families of those killed by the bomb on that day, and the third is made of memory pieces from citizens of the county. Some are written as unadorned statement; others are reflective.

To make the families' task easier, I presented a selection of poetry for them, one which might reflect their thoughts and from which they could choose. While reading for this I marvelled again at the integrity of some poems, how they cannot be bent to a purpose. In pursuit of the third section, I spent time in Monaghan Arts Office where people dropped in to talk. Some came simply to welcome me, some to discuss written pieces, and yet others to talk but not write. Indeed some came to talk with the strict proviso that I not write or refer to anything spoken about. This latter particularly applied to people involved in public service that day and who are still conscious of how some people have suffered and how unintentional carelessness of description could hurt, even thirty years later.

Certain threads ran through many of the conversations: how lives had been changed for ever; how the face of the town had altered; how, in shock, people had pulled together; the grim task of the rescue work; the extraordinary work of the staff of Monaghan County Hospital. But then silence. This silence has compounded the hurt of the day and is referred to by several of the contributors here. It was a constant theme of conversation. As if I hadn't known, I was reminded that a public court case or enquiry is not simply about accountability; it is also about letting people know what happened, giving them the facts which they can then grapple with to the best of their abilities, recognising the part that reason always plays. The purpose of this is not merely to satisfy the eternal curiosity of the history student within us all; it is a right, particularly for the bereaved and injured; and it is essential in order to curb the growth of rumour, which flourishes in a state of ignorance.

At the beginning of this work, a public meeting was held in the Hillgrove Hotel in order to put before the people the shape of Ciarán Ó Cearnaigh's sculpture and the proposed outline of this book. The discussions that took place around the tables when the business of the meeting had been concluded are what made this a unique event. It became, in fact, a tentative invitation to cast back, remember and discuss. Publicly. The room was full of people who talked and listened to each other. Some had not met since that day, which seems remarkable in such a small place. But then the circumstances of the bomb had obviously made people reticent and afraid to broach their memories in the intervening years. One man approached a woman and reminded her that he had gone upstairs with her in her home to get sheets and blankets. He wondered if she remembered. She did. Some, including medical personnel, talked about the reasons that prevented them from describing the day.

I mention these things only to point to the difficulties that this book sometimes faced. Normally an anthology gets an early definition, and although slight expansion or minor direction change can happen, it usually appears more or less as originally perceived. This was not the case here. There was no blueprint. We are used to the notion of the solid structure of the visual as memorial, but it is indeed unusual to attempt to have a book play a similar role. Individual memoir had to serve as part of that but had to be placed in the larger context of Monaghan as it was, and now is. Inevitably I had to make choices as to what fitted into the overall picture. There is a notion of town, going into town, going into the town, downtown, uptown, down the town, and although generally all is not as the playwright Thornton Wilder would have us believe in his play *Our Town*, all towns do have some features in common. Town goes beyond mere commerce; it is a place where the houses are up beside each other, yet the people carve out their own privacies. It is a delicate balancing act, one that suffers a terrible skewing for a long time if something drastic happens to it. Public recognition of that plays a part in the task of moving on, and I suppose this anthology is, retrospectively, part of that recognition.

The section given to the families was particularly hard for some people. They had to revisit a time that they have dealt with in their own unique ways. They have chosen to remember again in different ways. Most of the interviews with the relatives of the seven people who died are taken from Don Mullan's book, *The Dublin and Monaghan Bombings* (Wolfhound Press, 2000). Both Iris Boyd and Marie Coyle have penned their own lines, and for others I have chosen what I hope is an appropriate poem. I was particularly struck when dealing with family members just what a burden it is to be for ever cast as the relative of someone killed so publicly on a particular day. It is as if the personal grief one feels becomes public property. Again, I thank them.

The people who wrote did so at a cost. Some started and then decided not to continue, either because it was too painful or because they didn't trust their own memories. When people talked, they did so, obviously, from their position on that day, and also from the point of view of the effect it had on them, not always directly linked to the importance in their lives then. Often it was later events that influenced their particular perception. I was sometimes astonished by the stories told to me during the course of compiling this book. It was silly of me to be surprised at how many people knew the exact spot they were in when they heard the noise or the news. I was far away, handing out election leaflets in Mount Isa, a desert town in the outback of Australia. A Danish miner came up to me with the news. I remember being puzzled that he knew where I came from. Such was our lack of use of telephonic communication at the time, I didn't phone home; I waited instead for a letter.

Researching poetry, prose and non-fiction for this anthology, I thought a lot about memorials. The written word has sometimes played an essential part. The First World War poets immediately spring to mind, as do the sculptures carved in the trenches by Henri Gaudier-Brzeska—we know of the latter only through letters. Although some of this work is decidedly and directly political, politics and art are mostly contradictory, partly because distance is needed to temper raw emotion and to avoid the pitfall of making art out of our neighbours' grief. Yet we're all glad that Picasso painted *Guernica* as soon as he did and that Grace Paley wrote her anti-war work almost before she'd left the picket line. Jane Urquhart's novel, *The Stone Carvers*, is a superb mix of the facts of war, sculpture and memorial building. That book's central concern is the building of the Canadian War Memorial near Vimy Ridge in France. In fact, art becomes the only antidote. Allward lives his life worrying over the absolutely perfect material for his work, while the men of war spend their time and money oiling up their guns for World War II.

More recently I know of an artist, Robert Janz, who lived and worked a stone's throw from the World Trade Center. He refused to vacate his premises in the days following the collapse of the buildings and continued to draw extraordinary pictures, mostly line drawings of his cats as they surveyed the scene. In the evenings he went uptown to friends who had electricity and faxed his work to the filmmaker Pat Murphy, who then made a film called *What Miro Saw*, a short film of her dog watching the faxes roll on to the floor. Art defying reality, you could say. This book has tried to mix the act of remembering with the acts of art as a kind of salute, and I hope it has succeeded.

In conclusion, I should say that I do not intend to draw attention to any one piece. Readers will take for themselves what they want and need, as indeed we do when we look at sculpture. I have included brief biographies of some; others are self-introductory.

PROLOGUE

Time to remake half-remembered things:
the road to work travelled years ago,
stubbled fields, skeletons of houses,
colours lost in yellowed photographs.

Such absences are lemon on the tongue.
Come, somewhere is a song that can evoke
a new entirety, can heal like poetry
used to, or a first glimpse of the sea:

that living tree that grew in lightning flashes
or rather was illuminated by them.
Still it stands, love as deep as widespread,
sensing dark and light, making them whole

somehow, in the bole of a leafy elm
or fruit run wild again along a hedge.
From every dying garden flowers fly,
they grow towards their past, towards the sea.

Ted McCarthy

THE TOWN OF MONAGHAN: A PLACE INSCRIBED IN STREET AND SQUARE

PATRICK DUFFY

OWN AND COUNTRY are two parts of all our realities which have negative and positive meanings for many people. Until a generation or so ago, contrasts in living standards led to townspeople frequently looking down on rural dwellers. My grandfather talked about the townies in Castleblayney in the early part of the twentieth century who referred to lads from the country as "yalla boots", which had the same connotations as "culchies". Yet it seems clear that town and country cannot exist without each other: they are locked into a symbiotic relationship which ranged in the past from the hiring fairs in the streets where the young country people sold their labour, or fair days where the countryside sold its products, or the shops where the town's merchants sold their wares and services to the country.

While the composition of town and countryside can be described in material terms of stone and clay, field, hedge, street and shops, with shape and size and locational characteristics, there is also a symbolic significance to these places, which over time has altered their meaning for us. The form and symbolism of landscapes is often a product of the circumstances in which they were first created: the plans of streets and urban spaces especially, the names assigned to them, and the public buildings and monumental structures built in them, all have symbolic meaning beyond their obvious materiality today. So from the age of a largely Protestant gentry with colonial and imperial ties, to the rise of a Catholic nationalism and democracy, to the dominance of commercial priorities today, different codes and meanings have been attached to the landscape of town and country.

Towns like Monaghan are different from rural places in a number of obvious ways. They are concentrations of people, perhaps some thousands (or tens of thousands) compressed into a small space, in contrast to being spread out over an extensive part of a countryside. This spatial concentration may make for a greater intensity of community identity with the place and space than in rural areas, reflected in such things as self-conscious pride in community evident in newspaper reportage. The *Northern Standard,* for example, can be seen as a (selective) record of the town of Monaghan's self-awareness for two centuries, with reportage on aspects of the progress and achievement of the town and its community. As with all urban communities, an intense sense of place is bolstered by formal institutional structures of governance: the town corporation (which existed in Monaghan until 1844), urban councils and chambers of commerce, all manifesting a pride in the place that is town, evident in reportage of council meetings, concerts and other social events throughout the past century and more. Up to several thousand people in any generation may have grown up and into this comparatively small territory of streets and lanes, and yards and municipal spaces: it is well and intimately known and remembered.

A staged setting

Towns might be thought of as stages, places pre-eminently developed for display, performance and show. Streets and squares are for shop-window display, for promenading to see and be seen, as well as for parade and procession on ceremonial occasions. They are man-made, entirely fabricated entities, in contrast to the more natural space and landscape of the countryside, constructed by the generations that have made their marks and modifications in incremental changes to the setting: boundaries, street layouts, even rooflines, once established, rarely change. And planning regulations today add to this tendency to inertia and limited change. Monaghan's physical shape has changed slowly, usually reflecting the economic and commercial energies of the community and the booms or recessions of the wider economy. Up until the 1990s, the old established spatial parameters remained unchanged—the Diamond, Church Square and Old Cross Square being legacies from the last big transformation in 1820s and 1830s. Only in recent years has there been a radical restructuring of the town, and it is now on the cusp of great changes as commercial and residential expansion takes over.

However, the innate distinctiveness of Monaghan as an attractive Ulster town with its uniquely interlocking squares and urban spaces will endure, although their original aesthetic achievement as elegant expressions of a past urbanity has been lost in a welter of traffic and car parks. This streetscape is a legacy of an earlier age which provided a platform for displays of political or cultural or commercial power and control. Life of town and county "took place" in the grip of Diamond, Church Square, Market Street, Hill Street, Old Cross Square and other locations, where shop windows, footpaths, residences, railings, monuments and public thoroughfares all represented transient expressions of passing parades of power, control and celebration. Its earliest focal point was the Diamond, in which was located the market cross, symbol of the town's commercial role. The market cross was used in the eighteenth century for publishing town notices; criminals were punished in the pillory beside it, and labourers at the hiring fair waited there also. As in other urban areas, Monaghan's municipal spaces were used for symbolic communal occasions, public spectacles of parades, processions, marching bands, flags and bunting, to demonstrate loyalty or support for party, creed or ideology.

In contrast to the display and spectacle function of the town, the extensive rural landscape is less "on show" and more of a workaday and less symbolic space. There are some parts of countryside, however, which possess similar significance: the gentry's demesnes, with ornamental buildings, avenues, vistas and monuments, are good examples of landscapes of power and status. Many of the gentry were also key actors in developing the towns as showpieces of their social position in an era of privilege.

The landowners of the town, like their peers throughout the country, were involved in improving their estates, and their towns and villages as windows on their estates. The Westenras, who became Lords Rossmore in the late eighteenth century, would have had extensive British and European contacts: while MP for the county, Lord Rossmore spent much time in London. These connections had impacts on town and country landscapes back home in terms of transfer of ideas on aesthetic taste in urban design. Rossmore by 1860 had an enormous Tudor revival mansion in Corlattan, and the estate was involved in facilitating improvements in the town in the early nineteenth century. The

County Monaghan Grand Jury met in the county town, and this also provided an incentive for inscriptions of status and privilege on the face of the town. Other gentry with interests in the town were Dawson of Dawsongrove, later Lord Cremourne, Hamilton of Cornecassa and Coote of Raconnell. These gentry and a growing merchant and professional middle class left their marks on the townscape in the later eighteenth and nineteenth centuries—in Hill Street, Market Street, Mill Street, Church Square and the Diamond.

Improvement in towns meant widening streets, replacing unsightly thatched houses with more fashionable slated buildings, encouraging imposing architecture. By the mid-nineteenth century, the town had all the marks of a self-important county town: market house, town hall, courthouse, gaol, barracks, infirmaries, churches, hotels, inns and up to fourteen different kinds of schools. In addition to its visible expression, like all towns Monaghan also has an invisible subterranean webscape supporting its landscape—a complex infrastructure of pipes, drains and cables which help it work as a town, which link up its buildings and function like arteries in the body. This network has evolved since the eighteenth and nineteenth centuries as the town's streets and buildings were improved and developed and as technology allowed. In the town's early days, water was supplied by local wells. Its governing authorities would have had ideas on municipal improvement and civilisation. Initially there was draining and culverting as streets were paved and cobbled, draining water and waste from roof gutters, footpaths and streets, and from the households and water closets of the well-to-do. As wells became polluted and unusable, water was piped into houses from streams and local lakes, though the water supply was not up to the standard of surrounding towns as late as 1895 when a public meeting was held to discuss piping water from Sheetrim lake.[1] Some improvements were instigated by local gentry or by the town's corporation; others were directives of an increasingly bureaucratic central government, mediated through more effective sanitary and local government legislation.

The Shambles developed on the edge of the town beside the river, which served to flush away the blood of the butcheries. Although an important part of the town's economy, its slaughtering business made it an unattractive public space. An account of 1760 presents a scene of urban squalor and streetwise locals, in the privileged gaze of a visitor en route to a social gathering in Dublin:

> We took the stage at Ballywollen St [later Dublin Street] on the first leg of our journey to Dublin for the coronation festivities of His Majesty George III. At once we passed into a large square. Our nostrils learn us, our ears tell us, and our eyes show us that this is the shambles of the town. Evil-piled offal and smoking dung are everywhere as our splendid whip [driver] advanced. Pigs-aplenty wallow in the gutter. Tinkers and hammersmiths ply their trades. Amidst the confusion a smiling woman, bottle in hand, sits on a heap of cockles, cheerful in gin. An ugly rascal jumps on the running board, fulsomely we are wished safe journey, one and all. A bottle is dislodged from the boot by the wretched fellow who disappears into a sea of ragged wretches. We are clear of this noisome place. We climb the hill. It is the Gallows Hill and eleven bodies hang on the gibbets like a good wife's washing. They are blown about in the wind.[2]

Efforts to tidy up the Shambles took place during the 1820s, reflecting broader improvements in the conduct of civic life and manners in the town. Many middle class inhabitants were keen to remove the slaughter of animals from the public street. The land agent in Carrickmacross, for example, referred to the horror and disgust of these public executions, often watched by curious children, and the slovenly way in which the meat was then exposed for sale.[3] The pork market in the Shambles survived into the 1940s and 1950s, with the river continuing to serve as a receptacle for blood from the slaughterhouses.

County towns especially came to represent the identity of the whole county, as the location of county administration for perhaps three hundred years. Not only does the town community have a pride of place in its town, but important events in the wider life of the county (and country) have been commemorated or represented in various ways in the public spaces of the county town. We can see how changing times, politics and identities claimed and marked the spaces in the town. Most county towns like Monaghan, in the eighteenth century and up to the Great Famine, however, reflected the aspirations of a county ascendancy class—"county society"—rather more than the ordinary inhabitant of the county. Indeed, for the average tenant farmer in Clontibret or Donaghmoyne in the 1820s, Monaghan was principally where the gaol (one of the most extensive buildings in the town in 1787) and Courthouse were located, representative of law beyond the estate boundaries. After the famine, with the acquisition, for example, of boarding schools for boys and girls and a new cathedral, contexts and identities began to change, though the pages of the *Northern Standard* continued to reflect a gentry and unionist perspective throughout the nineteenth century. By the 1930s, the new county hospital was added to a range of other functions of county administration which had arrived since the establishment of county councils in 1898.

Buildings represent different phases in the evolution of the town's setting, framing the streets and public spaces. The location of St Patrick's Church, for instance, reflected the social dominance of the Church of Ireland into the mid-nineteenth century. In keeping with its privileged social position (Lady Rossmore had bequeathed £1100 to the building, Mrs Jackson gave £1000), St Patrick's was built in 1836 in the centre of the town, just off the Diamond and presiding over the entrance to what was planned as the New Diamond. In fact this space eventually took its name from the new building itself, becoming Church Square.[4] The First Presbyterian Church near the Shambles was rebuilt in 1827, initially giving its name to Meetinghouse Square, which may have been an attempt to upgrade the status of the Shambles. However, the square was called the Shambles by the Ordnance Survey in the late 1830s, though it was still designated as Meeting-House-Square in *Griffith's Valuation* in 1860. It was eventually renamed Old Cross Square in 1875 following the move there of the old market cross from the Diamond.

In keeping with their more lowly social position, Catholic places of worship were situated on the margins. So, for instance, a Catholic chapel was erected in Latlorcan and rebuilt in the 1780s. Another chapel was built near the Shambles, then moved to the rear of the Diamond. A modest barn-chapel was erected in Clones Street (later

Park Street) in 1824, succeeded by the more elaborate St Joseph's in 1898. The building of St Macartan's Cathedral in the 1860s coincided with a changing balance of power in the community, its location on a hill overlooking the town symbolising a Catholic resurgence.

There were and remain many other noteworthy buildings in this county town, emblematic of a self-consciously important administrative and commercial centre: the Market House (1792); the Courthouse (1829); the former barracks, Belgium Square (late eighteenth century); the former fever hospital (c.1850); St Davnet's (from 1869); St Macartan's seminary (from 1840); Old Infirmary (off Old Cross Square, 1768); St Louis' Convent (from 1859); the railway sation and goods shed (c. 1860); the model school (1860); the police barracks (c. 1850); the former Savings Bank (1855); the Orange Hall (1882); the former Hibernian Bank (1875); the former Provincial Bank (c. 1900); and very fine domestic residences in Hill Street, Mill Street, the Diamond and North Road.[5]

What might be described as a modest monumentalism inscribes earlier narratives of ascendancy interests on the streetscapes and buildings. The Dawson Memorial to Colonel Dawson of Dawsongrove, son of a distinguished county political and landed family, who was killed at Inkerman in the Crimea in 1854, stands in Church Square. It is an obelisk inscribed with the battlefield names of Alma and Inkerman, and was flanked until the 1930s with a pair of captured cannon from the war, a favourite ornamental flourish in many Irish and British towns. Ignored for much of the past eighty years—indeed the siting of a brightly painted café against it in 1922 might be read as a statement of intent by the new order after Independence—it is currently undergoing conservation. The Rossmore monument, incorporating a drinking trough and weathercock, was erected about 1875 as a Rossmore family memorial. Occupying a key location in the middle of the Diamond, it displaced the older, unfashionable Market Cross, which was moved to the Shambles. Though their significance has now receded, they are important parts of the iconography and history of the street spaces in the town. The Market House, which has been described as "one of the most delicate and elegant eighteenth-century buildings in the North", was built in 1792 as a facility and symbol of commerce and progress for the inhabitants of the town.

There are hints of forgotten imperial narratives evident in the iconography of St Patrick's Church: an 1842 memorial to Charles Westenra, missing in action in India, 1824; a memorial with drum, cannon, spears and bayonet to Captain Lucas, killed at Ferozeshah (India) in 1845; to H. C. J. Lloyd, killed at Isandula (southern Africa) in 1879. Finally, the Courthouse (built in the early 1830s) has a large coat of arms of the royal House of Hanover carved on its pediment overlooking the Church Square and its historic monuments.

Spectacle and parade

Throughout the past couple of centuries, the town and its public spaces have formed the symbolic site for a variety of performances which have marked changes in power politics and popular causes. Marching in procession, with banners, bands and oratory, has always been a feature of the use of urban spaces. Monaghan town's Diamond and Church Square have been used as premier ceremonial spaces, appropriated by different groups to mark their ascendancy down through the generations in local and county society.

A short survey of major public events in the town over the past couple of centuries illustrates the manner in which the town has been used for what might be called public performances of power, celebration or populist issues. Most of the record comes from the pages of the *Northern Standard*, which was very much a voice of the ascendancy and unionism in the nineteenth century; by the 1930s it had changed its editorial policy substantially to reflect the new social and political order. The usage of the streets for show and display was not necessarily confined to official or formal demonstration. More ordinary groups, such as local sporting clubs, sometimes took the opportunity to parade through the town, as when the supporters and players of Cremartin Shamrocks, travelling to the sports in Threemilehouse in June 1936, dismounted from the lorry in Monaghan and marched with a pipe band through the town.[6]

In the 1826 general election, Henry Westenra, son of Lord Rossmore, was elected to Westminster with E. P. Shirley. Nominations for the election were lodged in the Courthouse, then located in the Diamond, on 24 June, which was subsequently called Stoney Saturday in memory of the riot which ensued. Contemporary accounts mark an early use of the town's primary public spaces in demonstrations of political influence:

> At twelve o'clock Mr. Westenra made his entry into the town accompanied by five or six hundred men equipped with newly-cut sticks and wearing a green sprig in their hats. In front of the procession a mounted man bore the tree of liberty followed by one hundred mounted men. At the end of the marching file of men a small band of musicians preceded the candidate, Mr. Westenra, who was borne in his carriage by enthusiastic supporters. The party proceeded twice around the Diamond . . . The horse police were scattered through the excited crowds in vain trying with the flat of their swords to disperse them. The attention of all was suddenly directed on Glaslough Street as Leslie accompanied by Shirley rode into the Diamond amid the tenants from the Glaslough area. As the crowds surged into the Diamond small squabbles ended in a bitter conflict between the Leslie and Westenra factions . . . For some time the horse police tried to resist the tenants as the battle raged in the centre of the Diamond. Some stones were thrown at this stage . . . Under the order of a magistrate shots were fired at the multitude without reading the riot act or giving any previous warning. The crowds retired leaving three of their followers stretched on the ground and many among them wounded. The three men later died of their wound . . .[7]

Because Monaghan town was on a religious-political boundary, it became a sort of touchstone of regional tensions in south Ulster which escalated in the later decades of the nineteenth century. In 1861, 35 per cent of the town and parish population (8988) was Protestant, equally divided between Church of Ireland and Presbyterian communities. As nationalist influence rose, the Orange Order strengthened in the county, and in elections from the 1860s to 1880s the town, as the election headquarters, became a stage for sectarian demonstration. The 1868 election was celebrated in verse:

The Monaghan men in rank and file came marching up the street,
With young James Clarke their foremost, the Clones men to meet.
And when they met upon the spot they gave three hearty cheers,
For Madden our bold leader and the Dartry volunteers.
If you had seen their forces as they marched into the square,
No Fenian mob or "Midnight Man" to show their faces dare.
The rebel mob of Monaghan, before them they did fly,
For well did they remember the Thirteenth of July.[8]

There were other less contentious public demonstrations of communal pride by the town's community. In 1831 the laying of the foundation stone for St Patrick's Church provided an opportunity for ostentatious spectacle in New Diamond, starring the Lord Lieutenant "attended by the gentlemen of the committee and a large concourse of the respectable parishioners of all religious sects . . ."[9] In March 1840, Fr Mathew held a large meeting in the Plantation where *c.* 40,000 people allegedly took the pledge not to drink alcohol. Later in 1896, the incoming Lord Lieutenant again travelled from Dublin for the opening of Monaghan Infirmary, an important institutional addition to the town's services, and the flag-bedecked streets and ceremonial parading was probably one of the last public tributes in Monaghan to a representative of the crown in Ireland.[10] The *Northern Standard* contained regular reports on the annual training of the Royal Irish Fusiliers, who occasionally paraded from the barracks: in June 1890, for example, it reported that:

> Our county regiment, which has been up for training since 27inst will be all discharged today . . . On Thursday last the inspecting officer, Col. Hopton commanding the 87th Regimental District, arrived on the 11 am train from Armagh and at once proceeded to inspect the Regiment in the drill ground at Blackwater vale meadows . . .[11]

A last attempt at possession of the streets was made by the old order in June 1921 following the sudden arrival of a large military force:

> . . . there were large numbers of military lorries with them, and even an aeroplane. The lorries parked at the

RIC barracks and the troops bivouacked at certain points in the neighbourhood of the town on the western side. The aeroplane was housed in a hangar at Camla, beside Rossmore Park. During the weekend the roads in the area were a constant scene of military activity. Motor lorries, Crossley tenders, horsed limbers, motor cyclists, ambulance cars and an armoured car were all passing to and fro between Monaghan and the various camps. Soldiers off duty visited the town in large numbers and Monaghan had the appearance of a town in the war zone of France in the Great War. The military on Sunday night entered the post office and ensured that telephonic communications could not be used.[12]

Theo McMahon's *Old Monaghan 1785–1995* contains some of the last photographs of the British army parading in the Diamond in 1920.

The increase in what was called "party feeling" in the later decades of the nineteenth century was evident in marches and parades staking claims over the public streets. The Orange Order was especially noteworthy, with extensive reportage of the Twelfth of July commemorations:

> In Monaghan from 9 o'clock in the morning, well-dressed excursionists commenced to arrive, and by eleven o'clock large numbers were in town waiting for the several lodges to form in procession, previous to proceeding to the place of meeting. At about twelve o'clock the several lodges from Monaghan, Castleblayney, Clontibret, Ballinode, Smithborough and surrounding districts having arrived, they then proceeded with the several bands to the North Road and shortly afterwards . . . to Mr. Henderson's very picturesque demesne, where in a portion of the park within view of that gentleman's strikingly handsome residence, a large platform was erected . . . the Monaghan contingent was in itself a very imposing procession of well-dressed and well-to-do people, representative principally of the farming and industrial classes.[13]

Tensions arose as the balance of power shifted, however, and other groups were laying claim to the streets. One such demonstration was indignantly reported in 1885:

> The open desecration of the Sabbath has seldom been practised under the suspension and sanction of the Police authorities as far north as Monaghan but on Sunday last the peace and quietness of our town was disturbed by a band of nationalists from Castleblayney. Not content with disturbing the peace of private dwellings these scoffers at religion and religious feelings played when passing the Presbyterian church gate and stopped outside it while evening service was being conducted.[14]

The subsequent dominant influence of the Catholic community was presaged in the post-famine decades with the establishment of boarding schools in Louisville and St Macartan's College. The St Louis school was especially significant into the twentieth century in cultural terms, establishing a reputation for top class concerts which boosted the morale and self-image of the urban community. St Macartan's Cathedral was an especially significant addition to the built landscape of the town and to the social ascendancy of the Catholic community. An imposing architectural statement symbolically adorning a hill dominating the town:

> The ceremony of laying the foundation stone was performed by the bishop in the presence of all the prelates of Ireland on 18 June 1861 . . . and the sinkings for the foundation were carried on most vigorously. It was not, I have been told, unusual to see 400 or 500 horses and carts, filled with lime, stone and sand, arrive at the building together—the horses and carts and the men having been supplied gratuitously by the people of the various parishes surrounding.[15]

From the 1920s, the Catholic community had gained in self-confidence. My father remembers processions through the streets of the town by both schools for Easter religious ceremonies in 1928:

25

We used to march in procession [from St Macartan's College] into Monaghan to take part in the Easter ceremonies at the Cathedral. The convent girls would be there too but they had not as far to walk as we had. I remember once when we had come up Glaslough Street, the girls were coming into the Diamond at the same time. We broke ranks and mingled with the girls and Fr McGahan who was in charge of us went wild and rushed up and down waving his stick to try to separate us . . .[16]

This spirit of Catholic triumphalism peaked during the Eucharistic Congress in 1932, when Monaghan was reported as being "resplendent with flags, bunting and arches" in decorative schemes which commenced in Old Cross Square:

In a few nights the wide thoroughfare was transformed from the end of Dublin Street to the head of the Pound Hill. The Old Cross was converted into an altar which at night is profusely illuminated and before which public prayers are recited . . . Every house in the Square has a little altar over the door with a little red lamp burning before religious pictures. Streamers stretch across the entire square. The Congress, Papal, Episcopal and National flags all find a place . . . the whole town gradually came into the scheme of decoration and on Friday and Saturday nights of last week, hundreds worked into the middle of the night . . . Dublin Street is almost completely closed in above the shop premises so thickly is it be-flagged and arched . . . Park Street has its profusion of flags and bunting, so has Market Street, Church Square and the Diamond. In the evening, crowds stroll through the town admiring the streets in their congress garb . . .[17]

By the 1940s and 1950s, the *Northern Standard* was no longer the voice of unionism, as the balance of power in national and local life had shifted decisively. The newspaper reported exuberantly on a Corpus Christi procession through the streets of the town in 1957, demonstrating a total appropriation of all its public spaces by the rituals of the Catholic Church:

. . . the annual Corpus Christi procession of the Blessed Sacrament took place on Thursday evening when the Sacred Host was borne through the streets of Monaghan from St Joseph's Church to St Macartan's Cathedral amid remarkable scenes of religious fervour. The Sacred Host encased in a golden Monstrance was borne . . . through streets resplendent with flags and bunting fluttering in a breeze that relieved the heat of the sun. Flowers and shrubs lined the footpaths along the processional route and religious tableaux were arranged in doorways and windows. None could fail to be impressed by the devote [*sic*] atmosphere that pervaded the town during the procession. As it wound slowly along the route to the murmur of prayer, the chant of hymns and the music of St Macartan's Brass and Reed Band . . . People from the country areas who had joined in at the assembly point in Park Street lined the footpaths and sank to their knees in adoration as the Blessed Sacrament was borne past . . .[18]

Groups of religious sisters, women's and men's confraternities, Children of Mary and Legion of Mary took part representing the various interests in the town's Catholic community. The State was often indirectly involved by the participation of units of the FCA.

New political allegiances also claimed the streets in large-scale demonstration. New flags and emblems, tricolour and papal flags, adorned public buildings and streets where Union Jack and military regimentals had previously been raised. However, public demonstration in the town reflected differences in ideology and allegiances between Fine Gael, Fianna Fáil and Sinn Féin, rooted in attitudes to partition and the civil war. Contemporary reports also highlighted the growing participation of women in these events: in earlier decades public space was a largely masculine world; revolutionary Ireland saw more women coming into the picture. In 1934, Eoin O'Duffy was holding large rallies in towns throughout the country, and in February in Monaghan:

From one o'clock detachments of the Guards paraded from the barracks and took up positions at vantage points in the town. . . . Contingents poured into town on bicycles, buses and cars and at one o'clock a special train from Dundalk brought contingents from the southern end of the county. A procession was formed on the North Road in which General O'Duffy marched with prominent local leaders of Fine Gael. It was an inspiring parade. It is estimated that about 1,500 marched in the procession and most of those wore the blue shirts. The Monaghan Blue Shirts fife and drum band and Clones pipers band discoursed choice selections of Irish music . . . A striking feature of the procession was the remarkable number of young ladies wearing blue blouses and black berets.

The meeting in Church Square was large and enthusiastic . . . the huge assembly listening attentively for over three hours to the various speakers. General O'Duffy came on the platform and was received with tremendous cheering and the blue shirt salute . . .[19]

As the parade proceeded from Dublin Street into Old Cross Square, it was ambushed by opposing groups throwing old horse shoes from upper storey windows.[20]

On 10 April 1953, the *Northern Standard* reported on a "Huge Assembly in Monaghan for Easter Week Commemoration":

One of the biggest gatherings ever assembled in Monaghan was that on Easter Monday [6 April] when thousands of people from all over Ulster thronged the town to witness and participate in the Easter Week 1916 commemoration ceremonies in which veterans of the five Northern IRA Divisions from the nine counties of Ulster . . . joined.

Over 4,000 veterans marched past a saluting base in Church Square to the music of twenty two bands . . . Crowds thronged Church Square to view the stirring scenes as the parade swung past the saluting base where the salute was taken by Mr. Charles McGleenan, MP for South Armagh . . . The parade proceeded up Park Street and returned to Church Square via the Mall Road and Dublin Street . . . Slowly the tricolour on the Courthouse was lowered to half mast as the Guard of Honour came to the present and all eyes were turned to the flag. Then clear-cut in the silence sounded the mournful notes of the "Last Post". Then three volleys were fired by a firing party drawn from the Monaghan Coy. Old IRA.

The monuments of the former ascendancy age continued to preside over these street tableaux, though in straitened economic circumstances they were in increasingly poor condition and were little regarded in popular discourse. The Crimean cannon trophies were hauled away from the Dawson monument and vanished from sight and memory in the thirties. In 1957, the *Northern Standard* reported a meeting of the Urban Council where "Monaghan Town's Deformities" were headlined, including "the North Road Dump, and Corner stones hanging precariously from Market House. . . ."[21] However, unlike Nelson's Pillar in Dublin, which was witness to similar displays of republican fervour in the capital city, the Dawson Memorial with its imperial connotations survives. The survey of the town's buildings heritage, undertaken in 1970, marked the beginning of a new era of appreciation of the built and cultural environment of the town.[22]

The "Coronation of Queen Elizabeth the Second" was headlined almost nostalgically in 1953, but an event which would have been marked ceremonially in Diamond or Square fifty years earlier passed off in silence in Monaghan:

> There were scenes of rejoicing and festivities through Great Britain and the Dominions and cities and towns were profusely decorated . . . In Eire generally there was much comment on the attitude adopted towards the great event by the powers that be . . . and in every town where there was a wireless set the impressive proceedings throughout the day in London were followed . . . Few people were to be seen in the streets of the town, especially while the Coronation service was being broadcast . . . On this occasion public celebration might be described as being "extra-mural", restricted to Crosses outside the town where throughout the day, the Union Jack was flown

on the Orange Hall as well as from private residences. In the evening a large crowd assembled and sang "God Save the Queen".[23]

A Sinn Féin rally in the town in 1957, following the death of Fergal O'Hanlon, was a harbinger of troubles to come arising from the proximity of the border with Northern Ireland:

> Despite the heavy rain that fell the Monaghan branch of Sinn Féin staged an enthusiastic victory rally on Monday night. Several bonfires blazed in various parts of the town and several hundreds, including young women, marched in a torchlight procession through the streets in the pouring rain. Three bands participated. A big crowd assembled in Church Square to listen to brief speeches interspersed with items of Irish dancing, songs and recitations . . .[24]

In 1966 the newspaper reported on the fiftieth anniversary of the 1916 Rising when a parade of 2000 was held, one of the last official state commemorations to take to the streets in the town:

> . . . members of the Army, FCA, Old IRA, Civil Defence Corps, the GAA, Red Cross etc took part in the impressive parade to the music of bands and beautiful weather . . . The town was in gala garb. Flags and bunting fluttered in every street with the tricolour flying from almost every house. Business premises featured window displays of Irish goods and bookshops displayed books dealing with the Easter Rising . . . The Military Ceremony in Church Square was the highlight of the occasion. The Salute was taken by Comdt John J. Fitzpatrick, an Old IRA man and brother of the late Comdt Matt Fitzpatrick who was shot by British forces in Clones 1922 . . .[25]

An alternative parade by Sinn Féin was held a couple of hours later.

The following thirty years of "troubles" across and along the border, which struck at the heart of the town with the bombing of 17 May 1974, marked a reduction in high-profile public demonstration.

Although lives were lost and property damaged, the physical and symbolic structures of Church Square survived the outrage.

Notes

1. *Northern Standard (NS)*, 26 March 1898.
2. P. Livingstone, *The Monaghan Story* (Monaghan, 1980), p 478, quoting from *NS*, 29 September 1963.
3. Longleat papers, Trench correspondence, accounts year ending 1 March 1855.
4. *List of Historic Buildings; Groups of Buildings; Areas of Architectural Importance*, prepared by C.E.B. Brett for Ulster Architectural Heritage Society and An Taisce, 1970, 35pp., and review by Rev. Seosamh Ó Dufaigh in *Clogher Record*, vol. vii, 1970, pp. 325–35; see also Theo McMahon, *Old Monaghan 1785–1995* (Monaghan, 1995).
5. Brett, *List of Historic Buildings*.
6. Unpublished diaries in possession of author.
7. Rev, Martin Cahill, "The 1826 General Election in County Monaghan", *Clogher Record*, vol. ii, 1964, p. 171, citing reports in the *Dublin Evening Mail* and the *Dublin Evening Post* of June 1826.
8. C.D. McGimpsey, "Border Ballads and Sectarian Affrays", *Clogher Record*, vol. xi, 1982, p. 23.
9. Brett, *List of Historic Buildings*, p. 33, and Ó Dufaigh in *Clogher Record*, vol vii, 1970, p. 326.
10. See McMahon, *Old Monaghan*, p. 51.
11. *NS*, 21 June 1890.
12. *NS*, 12 June 1921.
13. *NS*, 20 July 1889. In the late nineteenth and early twentieth centuries, however, Orange Order commemorations in the area more commonly took place in Clones, Ballybay or Cootehill.
14. *NS*, 31 January 1885. Quoted in Lindsay T. Brown, "The Presbyterian Dilemma", *Clogher Record*, vol. xv, 1995, p. 61.
15. *Freeman's Journal*, January 1864, reprinted in Ó Dufaigh, *Clogher Record*, vol vii, 1970, p. 329.
16. In Patrick J. Duffy, *Landscapes of South Ulster: a Parish Atlas of the Diocese of Clogher* (Belfast, 1993), p. 75.

17. *NS,* 24 June 1932.
18. *NS,* 21 June 1957; see photograph in McMahon, *Old Monaghan,* p. 170.
19. *NS,* 23 February 1934; see McMahon, *Old Monaghan,* p. 103.
20. From Francie McCarron.
21. *NS,* 10 May 1957.
22. Brett, *List of Historic Buildings.*
23. *NS,* 5 June 1953.
24. *NS,* 22 March 1957.
25. *NS,* 15 April 1966.

Acknowledgement

For further reading on the public and symbolic use of urban space, see Yvonne Whelan, "Monuments, Power and Contested Space—the Iconography of Sackville Street (O'Connell Street) Before Independence (1922)", *Irish Geography,* 34 (1), 2001, pp. 11–33. Theo McMahon's *Old Monaghan 1785–1995* is an important source. The photograph collections are especially valuable, as these preciously maintained images of long-ago days and faces help us to imagine and understand identifiable places in the past.

I wish to thank Sadie Murphy of the Town Council; Peadar Murnane of Ballybay; Francie McCarron of Old Cross Square; Padraig Clerkin of Monaghan Museum; and Grace Moloney, Clogher Historical Society.

A Brief Account of What Happened on 17 May 1974

Nora Fitzsimons

I LEFT MY home in Annacloy, Downpatrick, where I lived at that time, on a Friday evening. I was going to visit my mother in Monaghan.

I arrived at approximately 6.55 p.m. My son Jerome, who was four years old, asked me to stop in town because he wanted chips.

I stopped the car beside the Courthouse and walked over to McGlone's café.

I had ordered chips to take out, and before I received the chips there was a loud bang. The next thing I knew the café came down around me. As I turned I noticed a hole in the wall. I decided to push my son out and I followed. A man came along in a car and put us into it with another boy who had been in a bus, and he took us to the hospital.

All the time he was calling out, "A bomb in the town, a bomb in the town."

We arrived at the hospital in a state of shock. Jerome was shaking and did not know where he was. The staff in the hospital settled us down in the children's ward. We were treated for cuts to my neck and face; Jerome had cuts on his arm and head. We were in hospital for two days. We were traumatised for a long time after.

At 2 a.m., two detectives arrived looking for details and they took my car away. Because I came from the North, we were under suspicion for some time. An hour later they arrived back and told me that the car was outside the hospital. They asked me if I had seen anything on my way coming to Monaghan. They seemed to think that the car came from the North that day.

Two detectives came out to my mother's house and questioned me again.

From that day on we never heard a thing from garda or politician, which to me was a disgrace.

All I am asking for is the truth about what happened.

MOREGROVE

Where water's neither hard nor soft
Nor the weather heard of,
We sat down and scoffed
The inhabitants—herds,
Tillers of soil, aye the soil itself.
Wind soughs through an empty wood.
How come the fox-gloves?

We bait deuteronomy,
Torture and taxonomy.
Dying, they let on.
Trying, we knew less and less
Of their unkindliness.
Wind sighs through an empty wood.
How come the fox-gloves?

I mind that time when brother
Made strange with brother
And yet confide the heather
From hell for leather
In search of apple and oil.
Wind sings through an empty wood.
How come the fox-gloves?

Now, it's six of one. The loft
Brims both eaves of a plank
A long drop above beef-flank.
Someone said the combine coughed
At the water fled uphill.
Wind sounds through an empty wood.
How come the fox-gloves?

Hugh Maxton

MAKING THE MEMORIAL

CIARÁN Ó CEARNAIGH

A T THE VERY start of the selection competition for the Monaghan Memorial in January 2003, I came up to Monaghan to take photographs of the town. I wandered about, not really knowing what I should be photographing. I walked around the shopping centre a bit aimlessly and finally bought a chocolate bar and sat in Church Square. Not knowing quite what to do next, I remember thinking, "It's the last place you would think it would have happened."

The journey from the first tentative visits to the final stages has been long and a little formidable. The early stages of the commission with the other artists were uncomfortable, due to our awareness that it wasn't a standard commission. It was fraught with many issues. Aside from the obvious expected aesthetic elements, the idea that this sculpture/memorial was being made at the request of relatives and other interested parties required me to see that this had to be their memorial, not purely mine. There would be considerations which I might not have factored into the equation. Particular needs had to be met and long-held ideas had to be incorporated. The eventual piece would be a combination of many views. If I denied this, I would be fooling myself. I knew from that point that whatever idea I came up with had to incorporate the best suggestions from everybody involved. I remember thinking, "After all, these people have probably been building this memorial in their heads for decades before I ever arrived." If I just listened to what was needed, what has been hoped for, for so long, the memorial would create itself

And so it was.

Many issues had to be acknowledged. The memorial had to be apolitical and show no religious bias. The issue of the memorial's exact placement in the town, the scale of it, the sensitivities of the relatives, all had to considered. Most importantly, if I lived in Monaghan town, would I want to see it every day? There is no use in designing something for someone if you wouldn't want it yourself. Could I live with it? Would it serve its purpose of remembrance? Its "livability" was paramount. This is something often lost in public commissioning plans. Therefore, from that point of view, I was selfish and designed it for myself.

It was important that the memorial should be simple enough in visual terms, classically proportioned, not too much of its time. I also had to factor in that this would be a highly visible memorial to seven people who had so randomly lost their lives. To be reminded of this every day as you shop or walk to school or work would be difficult. The eventual design had to be poignant in its meaning but one that could also be able to be lived with happily on another level. To this end I designed a piece that took its visual references from its immediate surroundings. With these considerations in mind, I began creating something that repeated the verticality of the other monuments in the immediate area (e.g., the Dawson Monument). It also meant using the same materials in the vicinity of the proposed memorial (i.e., sandstone as in the Courthouse in Church Square).

Through all of this I settled on placing my proposed memorial on the most accessible site nearest to where the bomb went off. To place it anywhere else in the town would be wrong. It was vital to acknowledge the emotive and contextual power of the site of the tragedy. To place it elsewhere was essentially meaningless. I also felt it was important to place it on a visible site within Monaghan to show that the town psychologically and physically acknowledged the loss.

With everything in mind I came up with the idea of creating an object that I believed stood as almost a visual echo of the two existing pillar columns on front of the Courthouse in Church Square. Essentially my idea was to create a third pillar or "presence", to be sited directly in front of the Courthouse facade—an act which I'm aware perhaps acknowledges metaphorically the lack of closure on the event.

Having settled on this form, the next step was to make this form in some way function. What could it do? At an early meeting with the commissioning committee and the victims' relatives, one suggested desire was the idea of incorporating some form of lighting element into the design. This was something which I had already considered.

Through this suggestion I then saw a definite metaphoric use for this "third" pillar. The incorporation of a lighting element into the pillar would fundamentally make it akin to a lighthouse, a type of beacon, lit through the darkest hours, a feature to take bearings from, a definite emotional centre or constant, a physical praxis for relatives and townspeople. The memorial's presence will be an unequivocal acknowledgement of the tragedy. This, which is something I felt was an important element, came from the many meetings. That sense of the bombing being moved psychologically to the margins. An uncomfortable sense of unfinished business. Therefore its scale offers no apology. With this in mind, I hope in the future the memorial will become an accepted and enriching part of the physical and emotional life of the town.

From my own point of view, this project has been a rewarding and hugely affecting journey. I have worked on emotive artworks before, but nothing based on such a contemporary event. My main source of interest has been of Irish history from much further back. All of my work has in the past been based on historical narratives and how the larger historical picture affects the individual in history. I have always wished to discover these overlooked individuals, and place them in their historical contexts. In the past I usually researched through libraries, archives and parish records to discover and reinstate histories. Many of these people I researched had been ignored or lost.

The Monaghan Memorial, however, changed that for me. Here was a relatively recent event; the victims were not lost in folk memory. Their memory was not kept alive through vague factual reports or oral anecdotal evidence. They were still remembered, and the events of that day were very much alive and current. To find out about these people I did not have to trawl through old books or documents; I just had to speak to their sisters or daughters. So many people who were directly and indirectly affected still hold witness. The people killed in Dublin and Monaghan in 1974 are not lost in archives or newspaper clippings. Much of this is thanks to the constant work of the Monaghan relatives and the group Justice for the Forgotten. Throughout my research I hardly had to refer to any second-hand source material for the information I needed. First-hand information was just a telephone call away.

It was this accessibility, immediacy and readiness to help which made the design and building of this memorial such a strong and personal experience for me. It is the continuing living memory and work of all these people in the past thirty years which have kept the victims' names from being placed into history. I hope at this point the physical appearance of the memorial will in some way help that remembrance.

HARD SHOULDER

PETER WOODS

ND YET, FOR a while there, in the wake of that incident, things did spiral irrevocably downward. Diffley gave up the job in Wales and returned to London and we rented a bed-sit off Acton High Street. The landlord was Yugoslav—more appropriately he was a Croat, a people with an even more convoluted history than our own. He had difficulty understanding myself and Diffley. He saw no percentage in being in a foreign country if your every effort wasn't bent towards making money. In this we disappointed him greatly.

It was also all off with Sheila. I told myself that I had initiated it, something that was, at the absolute least, an evasion. I was in shock at the manner in which she'd broken it off. A good part of the summer had been—for me at any rate—an idyllic time, spent wandering the streets of London. I went home that summer and then went up to Sligo with her and got on well, I thought, with her family. Lonesome Tom left me to Euston Station the night I left for Ireland. We were early. I had already bought my ticket. He came on to the concourse with me and we went for a drink before the train began boarding. There was maybe up to a hundred people queuing for tickets, families standing in knots together and men and women, of all ages, on their own. It was Tom who pointed out to me how close some of those people stood to their belongings, as if those battered, cardboard cases somehow contained all of themselves. They looked like mostly the people who'd come over in the Fifties or earlier even. They looked like those cases defined them—a definition of perpetual movement with no particular object to it. The suitcase as near to an idea of home as many of them would ever get.

I had all of August off that summer. The weather was balmy. Around my own place the whitethorns and fuchsia were in bloom. The things you take for granted when you've grown up amongst them. An uncle of mine was back from America. He was my mother's favourite and for a while there seemed to be some respite for her, for the first time since my father had died she seemed happy. I hitched to Sligo across Cavan and Leitrim, through town and villages, past signposts for places I'd heard people talking about. Mythical places that seemed to shimmer like mirages in that August heat. Places that weren't quite as they'd been described, streets deserted but for a few cars, collections of habitations that hardly merited the name town. A single street and then you were gone. These were places that appeared emptied out, half-asleep, as if awaiting some event that would start them into reality. The memories of those who described them to me their only, real realisation. More of those people with the cardboard cases. I stood between lifts outside a pub sipping a warm bottle of Harp. There was a young girl playing outside a deserted garage up the road from me. She had her ear pressed against a rusting, galvanised iron fence, as if she could hear life's great thrum accelerating somewhere else.

Extract from *Hard Shoulder* (New Island, 2003)

The Dublin and Monaghan Bombings—Commemorations and Memorials

Margaret Urwin

INCREDIBLE AS IT may seem, for many years after the bombings in Dublin and Monaghan no commemorative event was held and no stone marked the sites of the bombings. It was as if the worst atrocity in the history of the troubles had never happened. In 1978, a small plaque to mark the site of the Monaghan bombing had been erected at the instigation of Mr Paudge McKenna, town clerk. However, despite the lack of interest from the authorities, there was one concerned citizen who had witnessed the terrible carnage of that May afternoon in Dublin and had not forgotten. In 1984, when the tenth anniversary passed without any acknowledgement from the State, Kevin Walsh of Ballyfermot began lobbying members of Dublin City Council, seeking the erection of a memorial. It was to take a further six years before the city manager agreed to examine the issue at the behest of Alderman Seán Haughey, then Lord Mayor of Dublin. Kevin's hopes were finally realised on the seventeenth anniversary in 1991 when, at a ceremony attended by the Lord Mayor of Dublin and several councillors, a memorial stone was unveiled near the Garden of Remembrance. In justified recognition of his contribution, Kevin was invited to speak by both families and dignitaries.

Dublin City Council erected a larger and more fitting memorial close to Connolly Railway Station in September 1997. The large granite monument, bearing the names of all thirty-three victims, stands in Talbot Street, the scene of the second bomb explosion. The original stone was moved to Glasnevin Cemetery at the request of Justice for the Forgotten, where it now forms the centrepiece of a memorial garden dedicated to the victims of the Dublin and Monaghan bombings and the earlier Dublin bombings of December 1972 and January 1973. Councillor Dermot Lacey, Lord Mayor of Dublin, formally opened the garden in September 2002, when an interdenominational service of blessing and dedication was held. Dublin City Council funded the memorial garden, which was designed and landscaped by Glasnevin Cemetery Board.

On the sixteenth anniversary, the first-ever commemorative ceremony was held, again at the instigation of Kevin Walsh. He and John Rogers of Cabra requested the administrator of St Mary's Pro-Cathedral, Rev. Dermod McCarthy, to celebrate a mass for all the victims. Fr McCarthy readily agreed to this suggestion and promised that a mass would be celebrated every year on the anniversary. In order to ensure maximum attendance at that first commemorative mass, Kevin Walsh, at his own expense, placed advertisements in the national newspapers and wrote to the president, members of the Oireachtas and Dublin City Council, inviting them to attend. Kevin's initiative brought many families together for the first time, thus sowing the seeds of a future campaign.

Two of the Monaghan bereaved families and some of the survivors became involved in the Justice for the Forgotten campaign in the mid-1990s, and shortly after the twenty-fifth anniversary commemorations, the remaining five families came on board. An historic meeting was held in the Hillgrove Hotel, Monaghan, on 20 November 1999, where most of the Monaghan families met together for the first time. A decision was made at that meeting to hold a service in Monaghan in May 2000, to mark the twenty-sixth anniversary. Despite the fact that seven of its citizens had lost their lives in the bombing, no commemorative service had ever been held. A wreath-laying ceremony and interdenominational service, organised by Justice for the Forgotten, took place on Sunday, 14 May 2000. One of the abiding memories of those who travelled by bus from Dublin was the sight that greeted them on their arrival at North Road. It seemed that the whole town had turned out, so large was the crowd. The prayers were led by Rev. Walter Herron while wreaths were laid by the families of Monaghan and Dublin. A call for a fitting memorial to be erected was articulated. The ceremony was followed by a very moving service at St Macartan's Cathedral, in which Fr Brian Earley, Fr Martin O'Reilly, Fr Dermot Harkin of the Montford Missionaries, Rev. Mark Harvey, Church of Ireland rector, and Rev. Walter Herron, senior Presbyterian minister, participated.

The music director was David Drum and the soloist was the internationally renowned singer, Belfast-born Angela Feeney, who resides in Munich. The taoiseach was represented by Dr Rory O'Hanlon, TD, and other Dáil deputies present were Seán Ardagh, Austin Currie, Caoimhghín Ó Caoláin and Seymour Crawford. Members of Monaghan County Council and Monaghan Urban District Council also attended, as well as the late former Chief Justice Liam Hamilton, who was, at that time, chairing the Independent Commission of Inquiry into the bombings. The readings and prayers were shared by the clergymen, while family members participated fully in the service. John Molloy, a survivor of the Parnell Street, Dublin, bomb, read the names of the victims, while candles representing each victim were carried to the altar. The victim of the Castleblayney bombing of March 1976, Patrick Mone, was also remembered.

The prayers of intercession were read by relatives of five of the victims of the Monaghan bombing: David McCague, nephew of Jack Travers; Sonia Askin, daughter of Patrick Askin; Gillian Law, granddaughter of Archie Harper; Elaine Coyle, granddaughter of Peggy White; and Anne Croarkin, sister-in-law of Thomas Croarkin. Rev. Walter Herron spoke movingly of his personal recollections of 17 May 1974 in Monaghan. Describing the scene in the immediate aftermath of the bombing, he recalled praying at the bedside of one of the victims and spoke of the trauma of the funerals. Rev. Mark Harvey's courageous and compassionate words of regret for the atrocity prompted spontaneous and prolonged applause. Fr Martin O'Reilly called on politicians to work for a lasting peace. Before the conclusion of the service, Marie Coyle, daughter of Peggy White, expressed her satisfaction that the bereaved families of both Monaghan and Dublin had been able to remember their loved ones in such a dignified and meaningful way.

On the evening following the commemorations, a meeting held by Monaghan Urban District Council appointed an all-party committee to consider the erection of a permanent memorial to the victims of the Monaghan bombing. Now, nearly four years later, it is heartening to learn that this project will reach fruition in time for the thirtieth anniversary.

Margaret Urwin is campaign secretary for
Justice for the Forgotten.

ON THE BORDER

It was always all over us
Like hay on our clothes and scalp
Like sand in our shoes and blankets
Everywhere we found ourselves
The border knew us as children.
And we queued for petrol, coal and briquettes
Bagged our Christmas drink in Cullaville
Sterling mingling in our change
Politics tangling in our lives.

We answered to the soldiers
Watching clay-faced men in hedges
Counting tricolours on the poles
Everywhere we found ourselves
The border grew children in its hands.
And we watched coffins on the evening news
Allowed more travelling time for the Gaelic match
Always stopped by men with *soccer* accents
And machine-guns and shiny boots.

We knew places by deeds and blood,
Crossmaglen, Loughall and Roslea
And where not to venture with a southern *reg,*
Our natural hinterland was not ours
The same green was on the hills
But its people divided over the years.
Everywhere we lost ourselves
The border found us out
And slapped our faces with the truth.

Shane Martin

THE NATIVES

MARY O'DONNELL

THERE WAS NO missing them once they arrived. Three caravans, three cars, a troop of young women and their scraggly children. Although she only glanced at them, not wanting to stare as she drove along taking the child to school, she saw a lot. Her mind became distracted from the normal minor snags in the day, to be got out of the way before she could go to the studio. The laundry. Dinner for when the child came home. Did the child have camogie on that day or was it chess? Sometimes she got the times mixed up and would arrive either too late or too early for whatever after-school activity she thought it was.

Factory art, she would refer to her work deprecatingly, yet secretly proud that her botanical drawings, so popular with American and French tourists, were reproduced, with a traditional recipe for bread or stew or apple crumble, on laminated tablemats.

When the child flung herself into the front seat every afternoon, she smelt of school, of grime kept at bay through disinfectant and floor-washing, of chalk dust and children themselves, with residues of sugar and stickiness.

They observed the travellers on the trips to and from the school. Since they had arrived, some people along the road kept their gates closed all day. There was talk, her husband said, of knacker break-ins. She admonished him for using that word, adding that they wouldn't steal from houses on the road where they camped. A few of the neighbours thought they would, he said. That was the point. You were meant to feel safe.

It seemed to the woman that they were never still. She would wonder about this to the child, at the layers of clothes being packed or unpacked, at pieces of carpet flung into the ditch on the opposite side of the narrow road. The young women would look up from rearranging the bundles, momentarily distracted, as if the clothes were some mysterious mathematical problem to which only they could find the proof. One, who seemed to be in charge, concerned with doing and undoing, making and remaking the bulky clothing, wore a straight blond plait that reached to the base of her spine.

Sometimes, walking up the road in the evening, the woman noticed five or six of them crammed into one of the cars, smoking, talking and convening urgently. At weekends their men arrived, nosing grey and white vans with tar-spraying gear into the gateway of the next field.

"Why don't they live in houses?" the child asked one day after school.

"They don't want to. That's one reason," the woman replied.

"What's the other one?"

"Er . . . more complicated. I can't fully explain it."

"Try!" the child demanded, echoing her mother when she wanted an answer to something and thought the child was being lazy.

"Oh feckit, child . . . they're kind of . . . thrown out themselves . . ."

She disliked explaining big questions while driving.

"Fine!" shrieked the child triumphantly.

"Wha'?" The woman glanced at her, slowing as she turned into the drive of the house.

"You used an F-word! Ha-ha! That makes . . ." The child rolled her eyes, calculating. "That makes fifty euro you owe me for F-words."

It was a joke. The child would fine the woman one euro every time she used bad language, and eventually donate it to a cause of her choosing.

"Okay," the woman answered. The child knew she didn't really care about what people called "language". Not in that way. One of the little hobbyhorses of the aspiring middle classes was to keep the mouths of children free of all casual or comic references to fornication, body parts, excretion or illegitimacy.

"There's no such thing as bad language," she told the child as they went into the house. She'd written it inside the child's dictionary. The hall smelt of dinner.

* * *

Fires blazed as rubbish burned. Sometimes it just tumbled out on the road.

"Can we help them?" the child wanted to know one morning on the way to school.

She had just met the gaze of a child her own age, who stood staring with vague blue eyes as they passed.

"No," the woman answered crossly. The day had begun poorly. The factory owner had rung at eight to say he was returning two pieces of work. He wanted a quieter palette for the foxgloves and belladonna. Most customers, he said firmly, didn't want tablemats that clashed with everything else in the room. People were into unobtrusive taste, he added, subtlety. Half an hour later, she phoned back and left a message on his voicemail, agreeing to redo the drawings and to water down her watercolours. She cursed with frustration at the magnolia-walled obsessives who were frightened of pure colour.

"They need nothing," she said firmly of the travellers. "They'd only think I was doing Lady Bountiful."

"Who's Lady Bountiful?" the child pressed, unpeeling a bar of liquorice toffee, her fine eyebrows dipping downwards in a slight V.

"They'd think I was trying to set myself up as better than them," the woman went on, tossing dark hair over her shoulders, impatient to drop the child off at the school gates. "Don't eat that when you've just washed your teeth."

Although she spoke quietly now, the child sensed incipient anger, put the bar away and looked out the window.

Later that morning, she tidied the studio. As she rearranged jars and tubes, laid out the brushes, she thought about her trip to Australia the year before and the various displays of Aboriginal art. Dreamings, these pictures were called. She saw some bland paintings comprised of white dots on sienna-coloured backgrounds, which were really a dissipated version of something else, for white tourist consumption. But others drew her in and made her wonder about the artists' lives. Some of the artists had Irish-sounding names mixed in with their Aboriginal ones. There was a painter named Brady, and another whose first name was—of all things—Deidre, without an "r". This was because the Irish and the Aboriginal people had occupied the lowest rung of the social ladder after Australia was first colonised and had little to lose by marrying one another.

As she made her way around New South Wales, Victoria and

South Australia, she recalled many familiar words and phrases used to describe the Aboriginal people. The similarity had shocked her. Four-letter foulness, contempt, race hatred. That was not all she heard, of course. Everywhere in the world there were pockets of people who wanted to make room and to learn from the dreamings.

She took home examples of the dreamings of Deidre Napangardi Brown and often looked at them. Deidre's dreamings—"Bush Banana", "Bush Bean", and "Bush Potato"—were passed down to her by her grandfather and her father. What the woman now wanted was to know her own dreamings, to bring them to life again in her work. She thought about the drawings returned by the factory owner, the taste of annoyance still in her craw.

On the question of dreamings, how could she hope to inherit hers? Did it matter, she pondered, that her mother had hared off to England in some blind panic when she was four and her brother two? She only saw her once, ten years later, when she had returned to the town with two new children, a new man on her arm and a gold bracelet, heavy with charms, around her wrist. He was, Granny Madeleine remarked bitterly of her daughter's paramour, black as the ace of spades, with children the colour of turned earth. Why she had to come home again, parading around the Diamond and Church Square, talking in a new accent as if it was normal to show up all romance and Mary Quant mini-skirts, was something Granny Madeleine would never fathom. But her mother saw nothing wrong. It was as if some score had been settled, some imbalance redressed. She was quite friendly towards their father, and brought gifts for everybody. Yet people had pitied her father, who never deviated from his routines and responsibilities, but worked and provided, with Granny Madeleine always in the background.

* * *

The woman realised she was wrong about the travellers never being still. There were, she gradually noticed, mornings of utter peace around the caravans, when curtains were drawn and nobody was awake. She supposed they'd been up late, drinking and carousing, maybe even fighting with their fists. Their sleeping arrangements made her curious, the question of who slept where and with whom, and whether they waited until the children were asleep before they did it. She considered how herself and her husband suppressed bedroom sounds in case the child heard, when they travelled beyond themselves, gripping the tasselled manes of lust. But why all the secrecy? Just as they occasionally told the child to mind her language in front of adults, indicating that she could avoid being judged if she held her true feelings behind her tongue, in her chest perhaps, so too were they teaching her another kind of secrecy. It was not the old, shame-filled kind. They were not prudish. But this subtler one, the shame of joy, was a descendant of the older kind and still lodged silently in the minefield of the loins.

* * *

When the woman was a child herself in a different part of the county, there were gypsies, tinkers, all along the road below their house. They lived in a house on a hill, and the tinkers, the Connors, lived below in colourful wooden caravans, reminding her of the Wild West and the pioneering emigrants making their way across America to a new life. The ones below their house stayed for years. They settled at the side of the road, where a deep quilt of long grass gave way to a Monaghan hedgerow of hawthorn, blackthorn, wild dogrose, sallies, vetches and lichens. Against this backdrop of seasonal hedge, they lived in caravans, their canvas tents steaming in winter when the morning sun shone on the wet hump which enclosed them. Smoke rose through a makeshift tin chimney, blue and wavering.

One year, they left for a while and the County Council turned over the soil. Poppies grew where the tinkers had wintered. She picked her first, mad-red poppy and brought it home to paint it. But she didn't know how to mix colours, and although she was pleased with her poppy, the clouds behind it were a disturbing blue-grey, almost indigo. This lugubrious sky was not what she had intended. Granny Madeleine had stared hard at the picture, her lips in a straight line.

The tinkers returned that autumn, and her father, who knew the Connors were sending their children to the school in the town, would not drive past without stopping to give them a lift.

A pattern developed. She knew her father was doing the right thing, the only thing. Nobody could pass by and let them walk in the driving rain when she and her brother were driven comfortably to the same place. In one way she did not mind. She knew the names of some of the Connors girls. There was Kathleen and Deirdre, except they pronounced Deirdre as if it had no "r". *Deidre.* It wasn't as if they hadn't spoken before to one another, because they sometimes did. But she also felt a distance the width of pioneering America.

The minute they sat into the back of the car, where her little brother also sat, she could smell them so strongly it caught the back of her throat. Smoke and damp, as if emanating from their pores, hovered richly, sending strong signals. Yet they were a miracle of cleanliness when they emerged from the caravans, washed-looking and with combed hair, often in plaits like her own. She pitied them their plaits just as much as she pitied herself, for hair-plaiting amounted to a regular skirmish between herself and Granny Madeleine, who grew ratty with impatience at her complaints and could not resist giving an extra, punishing tug if she did not shut up. It was as if she was plaiting hot metal and not hair.

The five-minute journey in the car to school passed uneasily. Her father would ask a few questions of the tinker children and they would reply. Eventually, everybody gave up the struggle for conversation and a profound silence settled.

When her father stopped the car, she would gather her schoolbag and slide rapidly away, not even waiting for her brother. The Connors took their time as they got out, then dawdled towards the school. Both parties understood that there would be no contact, not here. She would merge with her friends, and talk would begin about homework and who had forgotten to do their sums or who knew the *comhrá* for the nun. Somebody said that Minty McMahon was trying to teach her cat to ride a bicycle, that she actually believed it could be done. The girls laughed. She liked the walk past the stone-built houses above the convent lake, beneath the sycamores, and in through the gates. Sycamore seeds spun down like helicopters, and she caught a few and kept them to twirl them between her fingers.

* * *

Just as everybody had had views on the tinkers back then, the woman now noted how freely people unhinged their tongues about the travellers, letting fly in unconfined rage.

50

Sometimes one of the women greeted her with a nod of the head, but slyly. There was always a hint of mockery in the greeting. All settled people knew that and were used to it. It was the mockery reserved for the oppressor. The travellers expected nothing from the woman's sort. Complaints, perhaps, but that was all. Once, one of the men smiled at her as she passed, and she knew he was going through the motions of appeasement. Anything to keep the woman and her type off their backs.

She wanted to speak to them, but did not know what to say. They had all the material things, unlike the Connors of many years ago. But even back then, settled people had often struck a wrong note. Granny Madeleine once made the grand gesture of giving the tinkers her Holy Communion dress, only to discover it two days later discarded a mile up the road across a blackthorn hedge. Nor was there any point re-enacting her father's offer of lifts to school. The children didn't go to school, but sat in the dust at the side of the road, or they would roll in the field beyond the caravans when the weather was dry. Once, she spotted one of the women striking her son on the head with her knuckles. He was crying. That bothered her. But it wasn't as if she hadn't given her own child a skite of the hand from time to time either. Nor had Granny Madeleine spared the bamboo cane, which used to hang threateningly from a hook in the kitchen. Child walloping was a grand tradition from which the whole country had only recently been weaned.

That night, she dreamed about the travellers. It was a wildly comforting dream and she recounted it to the child. The child listened, her blue eyes shining, as she considered the woman's words, hands tucked beneath her chin. It was Saturday morning. The woman was drowsing into her coffee as she talked. She had been driving slowly down Reid's Lane, a country road even narrower than theirs. The hedges were overgrown with blossom and leaf, Queen Anne's lace tumbling creamily on either side of the verge as she edged along. Suddenly, the encampment was in view. But there was a fight, and it made her nervous.

"Were they drunk?" the child inquired.

"I don't know. Maybe. It was the men, using their fists."

But she nosed on cautiously anyway and suddenly the fight broke up. The men began to beckon her into their company, without mockery. The women were there, too, and children, and there was a joyful chaos to their movements. They wanted her among them.

"Why did they want you?" the child asked, chewing thoughtfully on her toast.

"Don't forget to eat your crusts," the woman threw her a look. "They wanted to show me their flowers. Nothing but flowers."

She laughed at the memory. Where, in real life, the travellers always had masses of clothes bound together, now they had flowers, surreal exotic blooms, vividly spotted, wildly striped, all extravagance and perfume. One of the women pointed to them, inviting her to come closer.

"But where did you get these?" she inquired, "These aren't Irish flowers!"

"Ah, Missus, shure we're travellers. We picks 'em up travellin' around," the woman replied. Her hair hung down her back in a blond plait.

She was satisfied with this reply, and blended into the group, as if there was no dark side to anybody's life.

* * *

A few days later, she stood in her studio, hands on hips, eyeing brushes and watercolours. The child was away at an adventure camp. Her husband would not be home until seven. As a last resort, she decided to go out and search for inspiration. Fresh ideas from the sloping fields and hedgerows. It would be a day for taking her time, for meditating on the way wetness and light created colour, and not the thing itself. The thing—the flower—was an object, a vessel to be filled and inhabited before becoming something more than itself. She packed a bottle of water, a sketchbook and pens, into a canvas bag, then set off in the opposite direction from the traveller encampment. It was that time of year when the corn was a tired yellow. Soon, the threshers would come, beating the seeds into the trailers, the clappers spinning loudly, like wings of the angel who gathers in.

Although she had seen all the flower specimens before, it was as if this was the first time she had abandoned herself to the growth of August, to catmint and woody nightshade, yarrow and musk thistle. She sketched avidly, hardly noticing the sun as it caught her shoulders, which her sun-hat did not shade. Then she noted down the colours, the hues, the subtle marks. If they wanted subtlety at the factory, she'd give them subtlety like they'd never known it before.

It was five o'clock when she turned back, starving but elated. It had, after all, been a good day. She had surprised herself. No sooner had she acknowledged the pleasure of elation than she sensed something wrong. Her pace quickened as she passed by her own gateway, instinct leading her, though she told herself she needed a bit of a walk. She headed towards the encampment, hearing the cries long before she reached the travellers. Dread-filled, flinging her bag to the ground, she began to run, her sandaled feet slapping heavily on the road.

She found them, moving, running, but not in the usual way, not organising bundles of clothing, not cleaning and sweeping the caravan, not hosing it down. One of the women tore at her hair; another slumped suddenly on to the step of the caravan and began to rock backwards and forwards, her face split with panic and keening. The men began to shout when they saw her, urgent with telling, one of them yelling into a mobile phone at the doctor in the town. The one who had reversed his van, crushing his own infant son against the rocky wall, crouched silently over the body. She moved towards them, towards the man, and fell to her knees beside him. His fist was against his teeth and tears coursed down his cheeks.

"Oh babby, babby, babby!" he moaned to himself. "Oh babby, the wee babby! Oh Christ! Christ!"

Her own tears flowed. The child was broken and still, already white beneath sun-freckled cheeks, blood trickling from its shell ears.

* * *

That night, herself and her husband fell into bed exhausted. The guards had been out to the encampment, and the doctor. Her husband, annoyed at the neighbour who shook his head and said what could you expect from a careless crowd of knackers, had downed a couple of whiskeys to calm his annoyance, and slept immediately. Every so often his body jerked. When sleep did not come to her, the woman decided to get up. She pulled on jeans and a jumper, then left the house through the back door, carrying a torch.

It was as she expected, the whole world still suffused with death.

They were all there beneath a ruddy moon, shifting figures around the bonfire. Two of the children fought over a broken tricycle. The men murmured. The women swigged on bottles of beer, shrieking, wailing, but their voices dropped as she approached. She plodded on resolutely.

"Missus," the child's father acknowledged her, his face expressionless, wiping his mouth with the back of his hand. The others turned to look.

She stopped. The heat from the fire made her cheeks prickle. She allowed herself to eye them, one by one, even the children. Now there was one less than when she had set out that afternoon; one had been taken as she sketched her flowers. It seemed to her then that she understood something, and her amazement grew and felt magnificent. They were like any bereft tribe, anywhere, at ease with grief under the August stars! For the first time, they did not mock her with smiles. For the first time, they were not watchful. One of the young women, the dead child's mother, sidled up to her husband and entwined herself around him, her face smeared. The couple faced her, lustful and unhappy. Inexplicably, she thought of her own mother and her ace of spades lover, remembering what she could not read properly back then either.

"Mind yourselves now," she said softly. It was a friendly warning. The guards would come soon, the Council would tip heaps of clay along the grassy verge, or boulders, and they would be pushed on to the next place, owning everything and nothing, bursting through invisible gates, settling into native places, dancing wantonly through dreams.

"Oh Missus, Missus . . ." the dead child's mother called out, mouth wobbling as she wept.

MEMORY

DANIEL AUGHEY

I WENT TO meet a Sales Rep in Jimmy's Ltd, a pub on Mill Street. I waited for him for about fifteen minutes. As I opened the door to leave, I met him coming in. He apologised for the delay and persuaded me to join him for a drink. We began to talk business, and then a news flash came over the radio about the Dublin bombing. As we listened to the news an almighty explosion occurred. The windows crashed into the bar. People around us started to scream, and we threw ourselves on to the floor. We waited in fear.

After ten minutes or so, we opened the door and walked out tentatively into Mill Street. There was a lot of screaming, shouting, dust and smoke. Someone yelled that there was another car bomb outside the post office right in front of me. People ran in all directions.

I made my way to the corner of Mill Street and the North Road to see what had happened. McGlone's café, in the shadow of the Dawson Monument, a reminder of a war from the past, was engulfed in flames.

There were several cars in flames in the surrounding area. There were two people lying on the footpath near the site of the explosion. There was a man in a car beside the Bank of Ireland, slumped over the steering wheel, bleeding profusely. We helped some injured people while we waited on the ambulances to arrive. I admired the courage of the local people with cars who assisted the ambulances to transport the injured to the hospital.

When I looked for my own car, it was thrown against the wall of Paddy Mooney's house. The windows were smashed, and there was a large hole through the driver side door where shrapnel from the explosion had entered.

I learned that to be delayed can sometimes be a blessing.

MEMORY

DOLORES McGRATH

I WAS A greenhorn student nurse home for my days off on that terrible evening and night in Monaghan. I had arrived on the bus from Portadown and walked up Mill Street from Hamill's, and when I reached home, my mother was anxious after hearing news of the bombs going off in Dublin. She was worried that my brother Peter was moving flat that day and could have been in the vicinity of the bomb.

Shortly after this, the bang, the noise, the confusion, the chaos started. My memories of the sequence of events are as confused as the scenes that unfolded. A garda car was driving around calling on people to get out of the area in case there was another bomb. We went up the lane to Connolly's fields but then didn't know what to do. When we returned to the house, I tried ringing the hospital to see if I could help in any way, but the lines were jammed.

I remember going down to Greacen's where people were scrambling with incredible manic strength, looking for any signs of life. After talking to an ambulance man, I went up to the hospital to help, where I was directed to female surgical. The ward and the corridor was crowded with patients and dazed people. I tried to help wherever I could, checking patients to assess the level of shock and injury. People were coming, anxiously looking for their relatives. The strain was very visible on their faces.

I remember being sent for a drug with directions to a drug cupboard, which I opened but couldn't locate what I was sent for, and feeling so helpless.

Later, I was sent out on an ambulance call to a man in Park Street, with a suspected coronary. We arrived at the house to be greeted by Fr MacNaboe, who told us that the man had just learned of his son's horrible death in the bomb blast. The ambulance driver and I checked the man and felt he was better off at home with his family, neighbours and friends.

When I returned home much later that night, the shock of what had happened really hit me. We tried to talk about all the stories that were coming in. My father made us (my first) hot *poitín* to help us sleep, as we were afraid to sleep in case the images would overwhelm us.

(Dolores McGrath's brother, Michael Clerkin, was killed in a bomb explosion in Portarlington three years later.)

LUCKY BAGS

Sometimes a texture like skin
slips through my fingers
or the stops and rattles
of one cheap whistle
pierce the tedium
with warbling notes.
Then again I know the feel
of that erratic compass
whose North is haywire
and the ball-bearing
circumventing always
a hole in the nose
is quicksilver and alive
and Made in Taiwan.

There is a man inside
who dances on my hand
with heat, a live show.
That one propeller
and the halved fuselage
never quite fly free
of their armatures,
and the spit, glazing
transfers of Rin-Tin-Tin
and the Lone Ranger,
bubbles the sherbet
in the corner of the bag
like quicklime, or my mouth
blowing up balloons.

Padraig Rooney

WHERE WAS I WHEN . . . ?

JOHN McARDLE

WHEN, AT THE beginning of the troubles in Northern Ireland, the news came through that police had invaded the Bogside, I remember imagining the terror of those ordinary people and becoming angry that this should go on. When I heard the news of the first person to die in the troubles, I imagined the blood draining away, the finality of a young life gone, and I remember the realisation that somebody who was alive one minute, planning a life, troubled by problems, simply didn't exist a minute later. In that time of innocence (or was it because I was younger?) I could imagine my own death in the death of another, my own grief in the grief of another.

I remember where I was when I first heard of these events, just as I can remember the exact place I was standing outside a church when I heard that thirteen people had been killed in Derry. Outrage and the feeling that somehow the world has changed seems to weld us into a place that remains for ever in our associative memory.

But I cannot remember where I was when I first heard of the Monaghan bombing. It was as if, on hearing it, my mind went into that place I knew so well. The Dawson Monument, Heaton's, Greacen's pub, the bank, Dieselec at the end of vision, buses pulling into the bus stop past the corner, people passing on tractors, walking with new spades. This was the place I used to pass coming in from Corcaghan or coming down from Liam Kelly's pub where I drank Erne Cola in the days of innocence. This was the street I walked with the girl who was to become my wife on the night we kissed for the first time. This was my place, and my mind went there and lost itself. I was there. That's where I was when I heard it.

And the people who were killed and the people who were injured were the people I had met in that street, the people with spades, girl-friends and children, people on their way. We could again feel their blood drain out, again feel the pain of the relatives. Over the years we had become inured to images of pain across the border; now we were back to empathy. Or we might have been if we had not labelled the bombers psychopaths.

I met thirty such "psychopaths" a few years later: convicted Provos in Portlaoise, who had made the most attentive audience we have ever had for a reading of Kavanagh's poetry. We stood around and talked after the show, drinking cola again, not because of innocence but because of prison regulations. They loved places, too: Scotstown, Dundalk, Navan, Letterkenny; they remembered the briary fields of Kavanagh's poetry. They named lovers and children. They didn't name to blame. It was as if they were coming to know that naming and blaming only makes us imagine we are perfect, that by making scapegoats we can only imagine we are healed.

If we had been able to avoid naming and blaming, the Monaghan Bombing might have taught us that the age of innocence had let us down. We had been taught a love too narrow, a love that could be proven by the sincerity of our hatred. We had hidden the original sins of centuries in an awful righteousness; we labelled, named and blamed. The simplicity of righteousness had obscured the unpalatable truth that good is often achieved by greedy, self-seeking people and that evil is often perpetrated by lovers. If we wished, we could label also the people who taught us that righteousness, but they were our parents and teachers and most of them were lovers too, trying to escape from the twisted straw rope of their lives.

Can we say then that the Monaghan bombers could have been lovers too? Maybe we can't. And if I had a close relative killed or injured in the blast, I don't know if I could either.

MEMORIES

BARRA FLYNN

MY NAME IS Barra Flynn, and in 1974 I was five years old. One of my earliest, most vivid memories is the bomb explosion in Monaghan on 17 May 1974. I had just left my aunt's shop, Donnelly's on Glaslough Street, Monaghan, with my parents and younger sister, who was two years old at the time. My father's car was in the Diamond facing the Westenra Hotel. I got into the rear of the car and was standing on the floor with my arms resting on the front two seats waiting for my father to get in. I was looking towards Low Patton's, which had a large front window. Low Patton's was on the site of the current Allied Irish Bank. All of a sudden the large front window fell out on to the street. It was as if it just collapsed. A split second later I heard a very loud bang. I distinctly remember the tiny difference in time between the window shattering and the loud bang. Glass was falling from windows all around the Diamond as my father pulled me from the car and with my mother and sister made our way back to my aunt's house. People were coming on to the streets. I remember at the time feeling more excited than scared. There was also a peculiar smell which permeated the town centre at the time. It was that smell and haze that made the situation more frightening for me.

FINNBAR FLYNN

MY NAME IS Finbar Flynn, and in 1974 I was employed with the Department of Posts and Telegraphs as an engineering inspector with my office in Mill Street, Monaghan, beside the current post office. On 17 May 1974 at approximately 7 p.m., myself and my wife and two youngest children were leaving from a visit to my wife's family at Donnelly's shop on Glaslough Street, Monaghan. I had parked my car in the Diamond facing the Westenra Hotel. My wife and children got into the car, and as I was about to get in I heard a very loud explosion. All the windows in the Westenra Hotel shattered, and glass rained down on to the Diamond. My wife and children got out of the car and hurried back to Donnelly's on Glaslough Street. Hearing the explosion coming from the vicinity of the post office, I was concerned for the safety of the people who were working there, and I headed in that direction. I went around to Mill Street and saw that it was Greacen's bar that had been blown up. I didn't look in the direction of the explosion site and focused on getting to the post office. When I reached the post office, which was just around the corner from Greacen's, I saw that every window had been smashed from the bomb. I went inside and saw that there were a few telephonists still working. They had realised the situation and were only allowing emergency calls through to free up lines. A lot of people had come on to the street and I met several employees of the post office. With their help I got a truck from the yard and went to Patton's timber yard and got plywood which we used to secure the post office for that evening.

The whole town was probably in deep shock immediately after the explosion. I remember people seeming to speak in hushed tones. It was as if they were all whispering.

The Seven People Who Died

Archie Harper, a seventy-three-year-old publican and farmer from the village of Rockcorry, was waiting to collect his daughter, Iris, sitting in his car opposite Greacen's pub. She said in 1999, in an interview with Don Mullan:

I T WAS VERY tough for my mother. They were very close and she had always given him great support. It's not something that goes away. It just becomes part of your life. Neither Christmas nor living in Monaghan was ever the same after his death. It concerns me that the media often neglect the Monaghan part of the story and seem to focus on the Dublin bombings. I also feel a sense of anger that twenty six years on there are still so many unanswered questions about the bombs in Dublin and Monaghan. My mother is in her late eighties now and I would love her to get the answers all of us have been waiting for for so long. Who planted the bomb and why?

Interview in Mullan, *The Dublin and Monaghan Bombings* (Wolfhound Press, 2000). Mrs Harper died in December 2003.

Archie is remembered here in this poem by Iris.

Would You Know Him?

And would you know him if by chance
He passed along your way
While walking in November rain
To the fair in Ballybay
And would your greeting be a nod
Or would you share some crack
And would you be looking out for him
When he'd be heading back.

Would you recognise his silhouette
On a distant Unshinnagh brow
The majestic movements of his team
In hand his whistling plough
Ah, just watch those shires dancing
Listening to his coded calls
And him revelling in their prancing
While the green sod falls.

And could you fill his listening ear
In the wake of a harvest night
From an aisy chair in the back bar
By the turf fire's soft light
With talk of ones that are going and gone
Store cattle, auctions, land
And who's next for the thresher
And who's to lend a hand.

Would you know him in his meetin' clothes
Heading towards the bell
Could you see him as the kind of man
Would want any man to see hell
He got the education early
Knew the value of a friend
And he lived the pages of his life
Knowing that one would spell the end.

Iris Boyd

George Williamson, a seventy-two-year-old farmer, is remembered here, first, by his nephew:

G EORGE WAS BORN in 1901. He was a farmer who lived on his own after his father's death, his mother having died some years previously. He liked field sports and was a good runner . . . having once beaten an all-Ireland champion at a picnic in Castleshane. He had a real dry wit. He liked everyone and everyone liked him, as was evident by the numbers from all walks of life who attended his funeral at First Monaghan Presbyterian Church on 22nd May, 1974.

His niece said

After the death of his parents, George didn't have the same interest in the farm any more. He was more interested in doing anyone and everyone a good turn. He was such a good-natured person and a gentle soul who wouldn't do anyone any harm. Often when he came to Armagh he would be out buying shoes, which neighbours had asked him to get. My mother used to laugh sometimes and say of him, "Your Uncle George needs a gentleman's gentleman to look after him." He spent six months in Canada once but returned to Monaghan. Laughing, he said, "They make you work too hard over there." He had a great sense of humour. When his body was taken to the church from Monaghan Hospital, we were amazed at the crowds. There were so many people who wanted to carry his coffin that in the end it was decided to just let his cousins carry him a short distance, otherwise the minister would have been left waiting for a very long time. Protestants and Catholics alike stood together to mourn his passing.

Interviews in Mullan, *The Dublin and Monaghan Bombings* (Wolfhound Press, 2000).

The poem chosen is "The door".

THE DOOR

Go and open the door.
Maybe outside there's
a tree or a wood,

a garden,
or a magic city.

Go and open the door.
  Maybe a dog's rummaging.
  Maybe you'll see a face,
or an eye,
or the picture
      of a picture.

Go and open the door.
  If there's a fog
  it will clear.

Go and open the door.
  Even if there's only
  the darkness ticking,
  even if there's only
  the hollow wind,
  even if
        nothing
          is there,
go and open the door.

At least
there'll be
a draught.

Miroslav Holub
Translated from the Czech by Ian Milner

Thomas Campbell, a fifty-two-year-old agricultural worker, is remembered here by his sister Mary.

THOMAS LIVED AT home with my late mother. At the time, I was working away and was only home at weekends. He was a very quiet man. He was interested in football, although he didn't play himself. He worked in agriculture and was very well known in the area. Among the people he would have known through his work was Thomas Croarkin who was also killed in the bombing. It was very common for him to be in Monaghan as he was that evening. The news came as an awful shock to all of us, but especially to my mother. He also had two stepsisters in England, Mary and Alice, who doted on him. My mother was too traumatized by the shock of Thomas's death to even attend the funeral. She never got over the shock and died six weeks later from a broken heart. In a sense she too was yet another casualty of the Dublin/Monaghan bombs.
Interview from Mullan, *The Dublin and Monaghan Bombings* (Wolfhound Press, 2000).

The poem chosen is "Tarry Flynn".

TARRY FLYNN

The scent of cut grass
Hung on a briar—
He sniffed through gaps till his mind
Was packed with twenty summers' memories.
He held the stem of the briar and wondered
Something he had lost in grief piecemeal to find
And now the lane turned round
Keeping surprises up its green-sleeved arms.
He was walking through a quarry of iron stones
That was really the tomb of a king
The greatest of all kings,
A storybook king.

Dark boulders roll over the magical lanes.
At the boortree that has a curse but also a blessing.
The grass and ferns have powers
If a man only knew
Greater than the witches of Hans Andersen.
A castle might spring up here . . .

Patrick Kavanagh

Patrick Askin, a forty-eight-year-old father of four children from Glaslough, is remembered here by his wife, Patricia, and children.

MY HUSBAND PADDY was killed in the bomb in Monaghan on Friday 17th May. A newsflash on the radio came on some time after seven o'clock. By then he should have been home from work so one of the neighbours drove me to the hospital, because I knew something had happened when he wasn't home. When I reached the hospital, one of the porters said that Paddy was alright. I knew nothing until the surgeon took me to one side and said they had done all they could for Paddy . . . I was in a bad state of shock. They wanted me to stay in the hospital overnight but then I had the four children to think of. The twin girls were two and the boys were six and seven. We were a very, very close family. He took them for walks and played football with them. You know, the usual things a father does. They really missed him. The next few days after the funeral was over we were just on our own. From then on there was just the five of us. Nobody came near us at all about anything. As soon as he was buried, people forgot about us. I didn't get his due pay on the night he was killed and I didn't get his pay until three weeks after he died. It was very, very hard. I was living on £25 a week for a number of years down south. I had to bring up four children on that, because that was all that was coming in . . . When my son Paul was getting married I remember he cried because his father wouldn't be at the wedding. This kind of thing happens, not just with Paul but also with the other children, regularly. They miss him terrible. I still miss him. People talk about the passing of the years and time healing all the wounds, but it hasn't healed my children's, or mine, definitely not. Paddy was hard-working and very quiet. He minded his own business and he went about his own business because he was a family man.

Sonia said:

What bothers me is that the two boys, six and seven, they had time with my father, but my sister and myself—we have no memories of him at all. We haven't even got any photographs of us with him. We've children of our own now and they're not going to have a grandfather and it's strange for them too when you're taking them down to visit the grave, you can't really explain to them why it happened because nobody actually knows why and that's hard . . . In many ways we have been the forgotten victims of what happened, it doesn't seem to be part of the history of Ireland at all. It's just blanked.

Sharon said:

My mother always tried to give us the best, and whatever we wanted, we got. She made sure we got it. She did her very best for us. She did very well for us. Nearly too good. You'd wonder how she coped because she didn't get any help at all. They didn't even bring her a bag of coal, nothing; she wasn't offered any help for anything so she just had to do it herself. Seeing how begrudging they have been, it was probably the best way.

Patrick said:

. . . I can remember the day as if it was yesterday. I was standing beside my mother at the kitchen sink and I could see the windows shaking with the force of the blast even though we were a few miles from Monaghan Town. I think Mammy knew straight away because she dropped everything and said, "Oh, your father!" . . . He was easygoing, that's how I remember him. It's very ironic that such an easygoing man would die in such a brutal way. He was a man who went to work, came home and looked after his family. Just an ordinary man and then—gone! . . . I would like to see a public enquiry.

Interviews from Mullan, *The Dublin and Monaghan Bombings* (Wolfhound Press, 2000). Mrs Askin died in October 2003.

The chosen poem is "The Dead".

THE DEAD

The dead are always looking down on us, they say,
while we are putting on our shoes or making a sandwich,
they are looking down through the glass-bottom boats of heaven
as they row themselves slowly through eternity.

They watch the tops of our heads moving below on earth,
and when we lie down in a field or on a couch,
drugged perhaps by the hum of a warm afternoon,
they think we are looking back at them,

which makes them lift their oars and fall silent
and wait, like parents, for us to close our eyes.

Billy Collins

Peggy White, a forty-four-year-old mother of four, who worked in Greacen's, is remembered here by her son Brendan, and the poem is written by her daughter Marie.

Restoration

I STOOD IN the massive crater, my head barely above the level of the street. Looking from that enormous orifice, my eyes focused on the defaced edifice that once proudly brandished the epithet, Greacen's & Co. Ltd. It was in that *hell* that I finally absorbed the reality of the previous week. A car, a green Hillman Minx, had detonated with such tremendous force that it ripped through the building's sturdy exterior walls, devastating not only the structure, but the lives of numerous unsuspecting and innocent individuals. This brutal act claimed the life of my mother, Margaret (Peggy) White, and six other people. But, it did more than that. It shook the very foundation on which my world was erected. It was an asteroid crashing into my perfect universe causing chaos on a cataclysmic scale. From that moment forward, 6:57 p.m., Friday, 17 May 1974, life would never be, could never be, the same.

A mother's love for her children is, undoubtedly, the purest form of human love that I have ever encountered. It is an unconditional love, an unselfish love, an unyielding love. That my mother's love transcended the excruciating turmoil of her final moments is evident in her last words to my sister, Marie—"Take care of my boys." In the midst of intense agony, her thoughts were of her family and their future. Senseless savage men may have taken her life, but they could not annul her essence, characteristics which, even today, are actualised in her four children and six grandchildren. While cowards failed in their attempt to destroy a mother's being, they did, however, succeed in bringing years of lament and in negating what would have been scores of precious memories. Thirty birthdays without mother's vivacious laughter and no mother's home-baked birthday cakes. Thirty Mother's Days on which to retreat from the constant unsolicited reminders. Thirty Christmas mornings without the blessing of experiencing a mother's joy and exuberance as her children and grandchildren revel in the glory of the season. Well-meaning souls, unaware of the poignancies in prematurely and tragically losing a mother, utter with a comforting tone that time is the great healer of all wounds. The wound may close in time, but the scar remains for ever. There is no cessation to the void. Still others claim that removing oneself from the immediate surroundings will bring healing. I once believed this to be true.

From the depths of tragedy often arises a quiet, unrecognised heroism. It was a difficult task for my sister. After all, no seventeen-year-old girl should have to impersonate motherhood for three younger siblings. And, to amplify the dilemma, one of the siblings was a thirteen-year-old who knew everything there was to know and then some. I constantly rebelled, often for no logical reason, and before long I convinced myself that I would be better off alone. Despite what I recognise today as sound advice, I abandoned school and in a few short years migrated to London. It was this move that I thought would liberate me from the pressure and stress of being "the oldest son of Peggy White". I believed I could forget the past and journey forward untouched by the events of 17 May 1974. What I failed to recognise was the legitimacy of my sister's guidance and how fortunate I was to have such a wonderful person in my life. To this day I cannot find words to adequately express my appreciation for her great love and the heroic sacrifice she made for her family. Although forced into her role, my sister willingly accepted her new responsibility, and despite receiving arduous and energetic resistance, she more than abundantly fulfilled the dying wish of our mother.

London offered an array of escapes from the reality of my broken cosmos. No longer "restrained" by a sister's love and a father's strong hand, I found myself engulfed in a world where drugs and alcohol reigned. For three years I struggled to restore order and rebuild what had once been my perfect universe. As I slowly submerged deeper into the miry clay which had become my life, the future looked extremely bleak. Then unexpectedly, on a beautiful spring day just outside Regent's Park in north-west London, I met the woman who was to change my life. Six months later we married and moved to Florida to start our new life together. Left behind were my deceptive, counterfeit friends—drugs and alcohol. Submerged were the feelings of hatred for the men who had introduced such chaos to my world. The universe once again had a semblance of order, a semblance of reason.

The more time I spent with my wife the stronger my love for her became. A few years after we were married, while reflecting on our relationship, I began to realise the extent of the pain my father suffered at the death of my mother. More than twenty years of tender love and togetherness abruptly ended. The very thought of living without my soul partner pained me to the point of physical illness. I began to recognise that the boundaries of pain caused by the events of 17 May 1974 reached far beyond my sphere. They not only murdered my mother, but they also killed part of my father on that bleak day thirty years ago. They ripped his heart from his chest. Even today, those responsible for Ireland's largest unsolved murder cannot possibly have a comprehensive understanding of the consequences of their actions. Sadly, however, the greater disgrace is recorded to the accounts of those individuals who comprise the Irish and British authorities who, for reasons or perhaps self-justifications known only to themselves, have failed to bring to justice those responsible for such a barbarous act.

In January of 1987 my wife gave birth to our son. As I held him in my arms for the first time, an overwhelming sadness unexpectedly engulfed me. Perfectly innocent and just moments old, this darling child was predestined to live his life without the care, the encouraging words, and the love of his grandmother.

Three years later, one week shy of the anniversary of 17 May, our daughter was born. I see in her the quintessence of my mother. Through my own family the wounds of 1974 are slowly closing. No longer are birthdays without Mom's home cooking. Mother's Day is once again a family day and not to be suppressed, and the sounds of Christmas mornings again resemble joy and elation. Finally, after observing my wife and children, I have come to realise the real tragedy of 17 May 1974. It is profound, yet it is as simple as this: a parent denied the blessings of watching her children grow.

Unravelling

Unravelling
the threads of time;
an outrage embroidered on to covert disc.
Unwrapping memories buried deep—
facts, repercussions, raw emotion;
no conclusions, no blame laid in any town.
Long gone faces, flashes, voices—
personal, but published because of fate.
All paled away in public memory.
Unravelling
the intimate pain of loss and living day to day,
while cunning fools make law a mockery.

Today Ó Riordáin's *spideog* sings amidst the clouds.
An elusive, philosophical spirit,
years in waiting
to unveil seven real names
clouded in the greyness of time;
waiting for the final
unravelling,
when time will echo its tale
in a world where the story doesn't count
where only the deed holds true . . .

Marie Coyle

Thomas Croarkin, a thirty-seven-year-old farmer, is remembered by his brother Jim.

I REMEMBER THAT night in May very clearly. My wife, young son and I were having tea. There was a tremendous explosion; the windows of the house shook. At that time we did not realise it was a bomb explosion. Later on in the night we tried to gain access to the town of Monaghan but it was closed off. It was at this stage that word was filtering through that there was a bomb planted in Monaghan. We went to my family home at Killyneill, Tyholland, where the late Thomas resided with his mother. Thomas's routine on a Friday was to go to town after work, have a few drinks, get a bite to eat and travel home on the nine o' clock bus. We spent an anxious night waiting for him to come home. The gardaí arrived to inform the family that the late Thomas had been injured in the bombing and had been transferred from Monaghan County Hospital to the Richmond Hospital in Dublin. We immediately travelled to Dublin.

This was the beginning of eight weeks of emotional and financial trauma for the family. We travelled three times every week to visit Thomas in hospital in Dublin. This was specifically traumatic for the late Thomas's mother, a widow aged seventy-four at that time, who made the journey to Dublin at least twice a week to visit her son. Thomas was critically injured. He had lost a leg and had suffered numerous other injuries; but he remained very positive about his recovery. He was able to recount to us his exact whereabouts on the night of the bombing. He told us he had a few drinks in the Ulster Arms Pub and was making his way to McGlone's café for something to eat. He was able to show us an imprint on his hand which he said was left by the door handle of the café. The café was near to Greacen's pub where the bomb exploded. To our knowledge the people inside the café were safe. Thomas was just in the wrong place at the wrong time.

The late Thomas died of his injuries on the 23 July 1974, aged thirty-seven. It was devastating for the whole family, but especially for my mother, who had never given up hope that he would survive. He was unmarried, worked in the local furniture factory and lived with my widowed mother. My late mother died in May 1997, never knowing the truth about this dreadful atrocity.

There was a cloud of secrecy surrounding the bombing in Monaghan. After the initial hysteria and shock and after the funerals of the victims killed outright on the 17 May 1974, it was as if this atrocity did not happen. No one was held accountable for this dreadful crime. There was no emotional or financial support for the families. This was in stark contrast to the bombing which occurred in Omagh a few years ago. Emotional and financial supports were put in place immediately for the families and are ongoing to this day. People were arrested and a person has been charged and the investigation continues. Most businesses in Monaghan county raised funds for the families of the Omagh bombing, yet the tragedy which occurred in their own town was forgotten.

The Croarkin family feel that the late Thomas was "the forgotten of the forgotten". Local history books named the victims of the Monaghan bombing. The late Thomas's name was not included because he did not die on the night of the bombing but eight weeks later as a result of his injuries. We also remember here the other victims and families of the Monaghan/Dublin bombing.

The chosen poem is "Tarry Flynn".

TARRY FLYNN

If one could say
On such a day
This man did what
The fates could not
Its following judgment set aside.
If one could show
How such a throw
Of a stone or a leaf
Had been the ever undenied
If one could keep the main
Road and not many a lane
That leads to full-stopped gaps.
Out to this field to wander again
The inevitable is the pointless journey, perhaps.

Patrick Kavanagh

Jack Travers, twenty-eight years old, is remembered by his sisters.

WE HEARD ON the 6 o'clock news that there had been a bomb in Dublin. Jack's girlfriend, Frankie, worked in Dublin so he decided to go into town to telephone her and see if she was okay. He also wanted to go to Greacen's pub to cash a cheque. At about ten to seven he shouted up the stairs to ask if I wanted to accompany him. I told him that I wanted to watch a film on television.

About three minutes to seven I heard a boom and I knew there was something wrong. We lived in Park Street, so we were less that half a mile away from the source of the noise. I ran down the stairs to my father and mother. The next thing, the neighbours were all out on the street. We could see the pall of smoke as we looked towards the centre of the town. The gardaí arrived within minutes and evacuated everyone from the street, as there was a car parked opposite the chapel and they were treating it as a suspect car bomb. Talking to the neighbours I said that there was something very wrong, as I knew Jack would have returned immediately to let us know he was okay and to check if we were . . .

We went in the direction of the bomb, but the gardaí had cordoned off the area so we headed for the General Hospital, but again the gardaí were stopping all but essential services. Don't ask me why I wanted to go to the hospital. I just had a horrible feeling.

When we got there, it was pandemonium. I remember running through wards and seeing different victims. I don't know how long I was there. Time stood still at that stage. Then I saw my other brother, Jim, with Dr Eddie Duffy, and I said to him, "How come you are here? Where's Jack?" He replied, "Unfortunately he's in there," pointing to the morgue.

I said to Dr Duffy, "'That can't be true." He answered,"'I'm sorry Eileen, it is."

We went back home. At that stage my parents knew in their hearts and souls but waited on us to confirm their worst fears. My father took a slight turn at home. It was pure shock. The priests lived across the road from us and were in our house when we returned. It was bedlam with people coming and going. The doctor came to treat my parents for shock. He gave my father some medicine.

My mother was in total shock. I don't think she spoke for two days. The next day the doctor gave her an injection, at our request.

She always regretted it, as she never remembered anything, even the funeral. I think she couldn't believe it had happened. She died exactly twenty years later, never having got over it. She aged overnight, and for years never went out unaccompanied. She never walked downtown past the bomb site.

My father talked more about it and about Jack. Jack loved sports, especially Gaelic football. In his youth, he played with the CBS and later with Monaghan Harps. He also followed soccer and car rallying. My father shared his love of Gaelic football and missed his company. We were and are still heartbroken. We had to cope but we will never get over it.

Interview from Mullan, *The Dublin and Monaghan Bombings* (Wolfhound Press, 2000).

The chosen poem is "The Story of a Story".

THE STORY OF A STORY

Its end came
Before its beginning
And its beginning came
After its end

Its heroes entered it
After their death
And left it
Before their birth

Its heroes talked
About some earth about some heaven
They said all sorts of things

Only they didn't say
What they themselves didn't know
That they are only heroes in a story

In a story whose end comes
Before its beginning
And whose beginning comes
After its end

Vasko Popa
Translated from the Serbo-Croat by Anne Pennington

On that Day

Nell McCafferty

I WAS SITTING IN the Pearl Bar, in Fleet Street, opposite *The Irish Times* where I worked. Many journalists and politicians met there. I recognised the sound of a bomb, being from the North. I ran out, over O'Connell Bridge and down to Lower Abbey Street. The guards let me through the small crowd. I saw a man seated on the pavement, slumped against a wall, below Wynn's Hotel, which is where many country people met in Dublin. The man was smoking a cigarette. There was a hole where his nose should have been and blood coming from it. I lit a cigarette myself and stared across at him.

Later I heard that a bomb had demolished the café in Monaghan where the bus from Derry to Dublin used to stop for tea. It's so much different when you can put a face on the person who is wounded or injured, and one of the women who used to serve me tea and buns was dead. Or was she? Certainly one of the female workers in that upstairs café had been killed. I don't remember photographs of the Monaghan dead being published next day in *The Irish Times*, and that was the only paper I read back then. Such were the numbers and frequency of death at that time, that if the dead did not make the next morning's paper, their names would barely make the paper the day after, never mind a photograph. The single exception was the dead of Bloody Sunday, 1972, and the coverage given them was because the British government had had its own citizens shot. I might here point out, as a journalist, that, though I saw several people shot dead on Bloody Sunday in my home town, including one of my neighbours, and wrote about the event next day, I did not name them. I had more on my mind, as a Derry woman in shock and grief, than informing strangers about what had happened to us.

This woman from Monaghan though, if it were she, was not a stranger. A ritual had built up between us: I was hungry and she gave me to eat, and, even though it was a financial exchange, there was an agreeable civility about it. The woman I was thinking of was pleasant.

We had never spoken much to each other—hello, great weather, rotten day. I'd be tired, sleepy, quiet; she'd be under slight pressure. There'd only be a fifteen minute stop, and she had to serve us all in that time.

The first time I came through Monaghan, after the bomb, the bus passed the rubble-filled space where the pub had been. I wondered, again, if the woman were one of the dead. The bus driver couldn't tell me since I didn't know her name. All those sleep-filled years since 1970, when I first went south to work and took tea from her, and I didn't know her name, nor she mine. In the summer of 1974 I bought a car. There was never need again to stop regularly in the centre of Monaghan. Nowhere to park, easily, either, given the increase in traffic and route changes. Monaghan thus slipped out of the public mind. The new bus terminus is away from the centre, and the café there is emblematic of the distance now between strangers and the people of the town. It's not a café at all, in that there is no chance to linger and no locals to meet, apart from the staff, who are too pressurised, trying to feed the grumpy masses, who have barely time to rush through. Often, there is no time for food. I think at such times of that unknown woman and the leisurely way we once were. I have always liked cafés. They figure frequently in movies, paintings and books, from Marilyn Monroe in *Bus Stop*, through *The Ballad of the Sad Café*, to the Hopper painting. Monaghan, in the café, before the bomb, was like that, and this unknown woman was a central feature of that society.

There have been more than three thousand deaths since the troubles began, and I could not name more than fifty. I never even met all of the fifty whose names I could recite. This woman is not among them. Her face remains a memory though, and her face is associated with a peaceful break on the long journey from north to south, getting to know the whole country, at last. She made us Northerners, shy and strange, unostentatiously welcome.

MONAGHAN MEMORIES

PADDY MACENTEE

IT WOULD BE easy to say that my memory of the Monaghan where I grew up is of a very amusing and eccentric town. The town was undoubtedly full of "characters"—for example, Paddy Clarke who played the mouth organ, sang and sold combs and trinkets in the streets and kept up a bitter commentary on what was clearly a bitter life. Another, our neighbour Lily McMahon, had a small market garden outside the town in the remains of a walled garden which local lore said had belonged to one Dacre Hamilton—a priest hunter. Hamilton, apparently, had got his come-uppance in some unspecified way so that his house, garden, progeny and personal history had gone to rack and ruin in penal times. Miss McMahon was not beyond letting it be known that it was she (or maybe it was her ancestors, the McMahons of Monaghan) who was/were responsible for the fall of the house of Hamilton. She lived just opposite our house at the Hill with her elderly father (a gentle old man) and a large and ferocious rooster. Miss McMahon did not have a charitable tongue, any more than Mr Clarke.

Captain Kavanagh ran a small timber-built café under the shadow of the monument in Church Square, dyed his hair or wore a wig (I can't remember which) and dressed in the height of 1920s fashion. He was believed to be a bachelor, but some maintained that he had a past (unspecified). Perhaps his "Captain" should have inverted commas, but there is no doubt the emphasis was on the second syllable of his surname. I was never in his café, and don't know anyone who was or have any idea who his clientele consisted of, but he made a living, probably eked out by his British army pension. Miss Doherty ran a lodging house in Old Cross Square, then popularly known as the Shambles (where my grandfather, a schoolteacher, used to live before his house was burnt and he moved to Emyvale). Miss Doherty's was a premises of incredible squalor. My friend Paddy Holland, who lived near by, and I used to try to look in through the back windows of Miss Doherty's establishment, but we never spotted a guest—and Miss Doherty was quick to repel inspectors.

I would not like to give the impression that eccentricity was confined to the poor—far from it. The Church, the gentry, the professions, the public service and commerce all contributed to a sense of living in a three-ring circus—which, no doubt, has left its mark. Neither would I like to give the impression that I remember Monaghan in the forties and early fifties as a "fun place to live". It wasn't—especially for the poor. I have memories of watching awful hardship, naked and systematic abuses of power, bigotry and intolerance.

I remember a very poor boy coming to school with a ringworm and being beaten savagely for "coming here in that condition". From infants' school I recall a simple-minded orphan girl (a gentle girl) being required to dress up as Deanna Durbin (lip-stick, rouge and all) and sing and dance for a class of her schoolmates who paid 6d. to witness her degradation.

I remember the soup kitchens of the war years and the two old men (probably younger than I am now) who came to collect buckets of stew cooked on our no. 8 Stanley range and the ranges of other members of the middle class and distributed by the Saint Vincent de Paul because some parents were too poor to feed their children.

I remember clever children having to leave school at fourteen to get jobs to support their families and ending up at dead-end work, on the dole or in England. I remember even then finding it difficult to understand why the two cleverest boys in my class had to leave school and I, third or forth or lower in the class and others who didn't even feature in the placings, would be going to university. Few seemed to even notice the injustice of this state of affairs or its obvious wastefulness to the country and everyone concerned. I remember classmates who joined celibate religious congregations, probably to get further education. What could anyone in their early, or indeed late, teens know about the meaning, let alone the implications, of celibacy. I remember the ravages of TB, which destroyed whole families—and had to be concealed for as long as possible. The first concern of any prospective employer would invariably be, " Is there TB anywhere in the family?"

I remember the mindless bigotry. The rules whereby a man or woman could not enter the church of a neighbour, with whom they had shared the same earth and sky and their common humanity, to celebrate that neighbour's life and its completion in death, were surely wrong and crass. But I remember my father and his friends hanging around outside Protestant churches waiting to follow the coffin to the grave but unable to enter the Protestant church and join the bereaved in prayer to the same God. I remember the bigotry and where it led and still leads.

But I also remember swimming in Lamb's Lake in those heavenly summers, and Christmas parties and the drama of Tenebrae in the cathedral in Holy Week; going to the railway station with my sister Betty to meet my father off the train when he came back from his surgery in Clones on Tuesdays and Thursdays. I remember going shooting with my father on Bragan Mountain (a mixed memory because I have always been a very bad shot). I remember the sense of danger and adventure when my mother set off during the war to visit her parents in Newcastle-on-Tyne and the relief when she came back safe. I remember friendships and enthusiasms and flirtations—and pain.

What I cannot do is reconcile these two sets of memories. The two worlds I remember do not fit together. I believe this indicates something seriously wrong. Is it with memory, or with language or with me? I don't know the answer, but it worries me—greatly.

Odi et amo et excrucior.

LIFE SKETCHING

Spaces left unfilled are as important as spaces filled.

In the Louis Convent, Sister Trea taught us still life
with the girls, watercolours, calligraphy; life sketching
was imaginative. Angela's hand lay like a glove
round the lovely bone of her knee between thumb and
    finger,
ankles slim as Ino's. I loved to sketch with the smooth coal,
smudge it just the right amount, get it just the way it was.

When the minibus came to ferry us back to the Sem,
I was having trouble with her maroon v-neck and white
blouse, a torc of shading between skin and collar. Outside,
we curled our fingers around slim rocks, sent skimmers
    skidding
on the lake. None ever reached the crannóg, where you
    floated
by a buoyant log, while divers plumbed and bubbled.
Patients
from the Mental, and the sleepwalking nun, and all of us
chant together:
    All art is made of straight lines and curved lines.
Aidan Rooney-Céspedes

Sport

Frank McNally

MEMORY CAN BE very unreliable, which is no bad thing. Sun-drenched summers and Monaghan football victories take up a lot more space in mine than, strictly speaking, the statistics would justify. And for all the horrors that that decade brought, for me the 1970s are still defined as much as anything by glorious moments in sport. It's a luxury robbed of other contributors to this book, I know. But in my mind's selective archive, the summer of 1974 is for ever filed under "World Cup Finals (West Germany)". You can measure your life out in soccer's world cups, spaced out as they are in well-defined, four-year intervals. In this respect at least, if you were born in 1962—itself a World Cup year—you were especially lucky.

One obvious advantage is that England's 1966 victory is merciful-ly lost in infancy, which is as blind as the Russian linesman who ruled in favour of Geoff Hurst's second "goal". Less fortunately, the great Latin carnival that was Mexico 1970 also came too early to be fully appreciated in your world, where Pelé hadn't completely replaced Santa Claus as the person you most admired. Eight years later, the paper-snow blizzards of Argentina '78 somehow mirrored the hor-monal chaos involved in being sixteen. But in between Mexico and Argentina, there was West Germany 1974. A cool, north European affair, which perfectly fitted the short, rational period between child-hood and adolescence. Gone were the beautiful Brazilians of 1970, with the poetic names—Jairzinho, Rivelino, Carlos Alberto—that rolled as pleasantly as the black and white spotted ball they played with. In fact, Rivelino was still there in Germany. But lovers of beau-ty scanned the 1974 side in vain. The trademark of the new Brazilians was their attempt to kick lumps out of Holland, the team that had inherited the role of soccer's romantics. The Dutch poetry took a bit of getting used to. It was all harsh consonants—Rep, Krol, Rensenbrink, Van der Kerkhof—you could cut yourself on some of the surnames. But outside of Germany (West), everybody wanted them to win. And yet, for me, the biggest disappointment of the 1974 final was not that they didn't, but that I ended up watching the game on my own.

As well as being spectacles in themselves, big football matches are exercises in male bonding. The 1974 final started well in this regard. I watched the build-up on television in the kitchen of our Monaghan farmhouse with my father and some neighbours who'd come to help with the hay-making: an event—I was dimly aware—also scheduled for that day. The dinner was over, and the television experts were assuring us, as if we didn't know, that this was the greatest show on earth, and that the planet would be suspended on its axis for the next two hours while the drama played out. The clock in the kitchen ticked down towards kick-off. And we were just about to join the commentary team in Munich when, on some unseen signal—the flick of a cap, maybe—my father and the other men got up and left for the fields. I watched them leave, in stunned silence. I could hardly believe it. The World Cup final! And these—peasants was too good a word—were turning their backs on it. No doubt one of them commented in the direction of the television: "That's all right, but it won't get the hay in." This was a popular philosophy in the Monaghan of my childhood, rivalled only by an alternative school of thought that argued: "That's all right, but it won't get the cows milked." Anyway, they were gone, and I probably should have been grateful that no one insisted I join them. But in their absence, the occasion had developed a slow puncture, and by kick-off it was flat. It reinflated quickly, thanks to the game's sensational opening, in which Holland scored before the Germans touched the ball. Fifteen Dutch passes, culminating with a run into the box by Cruyff. Foul! Penalty! BBC commentator praising courage of English referee Jack Taylor, as Neeskens converts. 1–0 after 80 seconds.

The Dutch masters are not masters for long, however. Inevitably the Germans keep their heads, and are back on terms when Holzenbein zeroes in on goal, attracts slight contact from a defender, and performs the death scene from *Swan Lake*. Another penalty. BBC commentator silent on Taylor's weakness for opera. 1–1. Then Muller swivels and rolls a shot past a Dutch keeper, who has none of Holzenbein's talent for diving and watches with the indifference of a goalpost, and the ball passes him by.

2–1 Germany. Half-time. Full-time. Der Kaiser—Franz Beckenbauer—lifts the trophy. The sense of betrayal evaporated, I could barely wait to relay the news to the peasantry out in the fields, where it was received with gratifying enough interest. Not as something worthy of serious consideration, but as a temporary distraction from reality, almost as interesting as the tea and sandwiches that accompanied it. Not as relevant, for example, as that dark cloud on the horizon.

I wasn't the first Monaghan person to wonder about the things that mattered in the locality. Patrick Kavanagh wrote the poem "Epic" about a border dispute between his neighbours in 1938, and included the line: "That was the year of the Munich bother."

Maybe it was something about Munich, I thought. But in a gentle way and not before time, the 1974 World Cup final introduced me to the concept of perspective. The selectivity of memory applies most famously to the weather. I could cod myself that the summer of '74, like all the summers we remember, was warm and balmy. Unfortunately I've checked, and I know that it was one of the wettest on record. The horizon was rarely without clouds in 1974; you made hay when you could, and it was still liable to rot in the fields. Otherwise, even Monaghan farmers might have taken time out to watch West Germany v. Holland. Whatever about indifference to the outside world, Monaghan cared enough about its own heritage to found, in 1974, a county museum: the first and still the best of its kind, and immediately the focus for school tours. Like most museums, it groups exhibits in time zones—the stone age, the monastic age, etc.—with their chronological relatives. But this is another area in which my personal archive falls down.

For example, two of the other great sports events of 1974 were the dawn of the Liam Brady Age, in the form of the Irish soccer team's 3–0 win over the Soviet Union at Dalymount Park; and much further afield, the "Rumble in the Jungle", between Muhummad Ali and George Foreman. Each occupies a museum of its own in my memory, the original exhibits fleshed out by details picked up over the years since. The Dalymount match was Brady's competitive debut, and he looked every bit the guy who—as I read later—almost threw up from nerves in the hotel. Team-mate Ray Treacy told player-manager

Johnny Giles: "Forget about him—his bottle's gone." But in the event it was his nerves rather than his breakfast that Brady left behind him, and he conducted the Irish team like an orchestra, leaving Giles and the rest of us as spectators at the opening of an era in Irish soccer. Don Givens scored a hat-trick, and RTÉ commentator Jimmy Magee captured the dizzy mood in Dalymount: "The crowd are chanting. They want four. Perhaps it's inflation." If it wasn't exactly Ten Days that Shook the World, it was an hour and a half that shook Russia.

The Ali-Foreman fight in Zaire spawned a somewhat greater legend. It inspired a hit song, a book by Norman Mailer, an award-winning documentary, and a two-year depression that started the transformation of Foreman from an ugly thug into the amiable preacher and seller of fat-reducing grill machines that he is today. Above all it was Ali's finest hour: up to and including the moment when he pulled his last punch so as not to spoil the aesthetic as Foreman went down.

Everybody remembers Ali coming off the ropes in Round 8 to win, and Harry Carpenter—who moments earlier had been remarking how desperately tired he looked—shouting: "Oh my God, he's won the title back at thirty-two." But my favourite picture in the museum is from the end of the epic Round 1. Ali breathing hard from the effort of throwing a dozen right-hand leads in a desperate, unorthodox attempt to end the fight early, and now steeling himself for the bodily punishment that would come with Plan B, ever afterwards known as the "rope-a-dope trick". There are no connecting doors in my memory between the Ireland match and the fight, and I was astonished recently to learn that they occurred within twelve hours of each other. Astonished and disappointed, as if the calendar detail stripped the events of their legend and returned them to the level of things that merely happened.

The gods make their own importance, and all that. Even so, it's a struggle to recall individual sporting events in Monaghan in 1974, maybe because they were too much a part of the everyday. We lived between the two football fields in Carrickmacross. Beside us was the soccer pitch, where the most exciting events then were visits from the likes of mighty Clones outfit Tunney Meat Packers in the Stedfast (STET) Cup. And where the heady events of 1993, when the pitch hosted Jack Charlton's Irish team for training sessions attended by the national media and a crowd about fifteen times the ground's capacity, were still science fiction. Meanwhile, just up the road was Emmet Park, where county finals were sometimes played, and the odd inter-county game. I saw Dublin beat Monaghan there sometime in the early seventies, but it must have been before the visitors developed glamour, because there wasn't a huge attendance. Of course, '74 was the Dubs' breakthrough year. It threatened to be Monaghan's break-through year as well. But as so often, the threat was narrowly averted.

The archives of the *Northern Standard* for 1974 claim that, as of early May, "football fever is sweeping Monaghan". I don't know. Either Carrick had been vaccinated against the illness; or, like the White House tapes that were also making news at the time, my mem-ory has an unexplained gap. Maybe it was a slight overstatement, like the paper's headline in January that read "Ireland Could Be the Kuwait of the EEC": a claim by a Monaghan-born Scottish academ-ic, based on oil explorations then being made in the North Sea. The oil optimism quickly waned, and a mere two months later, a member of Monaghan County Council was urging a turf-production drive to counteract the fuel shortages and the rising price of coal. "Back to the Bog" read the headline.

Monaghan's GAA fans suffered similarly dramatic mood-swings in 1974, as the county team performed on either rocket fuel or peat, depending on the humour. For a while it was mostly the former. A bandwagon started rolling in April when they beat Armagh in the pre-liminary round of the McKenna Cup, Ulster's spring competition. When they added the scalp of Ulster champions Tyrone in the quar-ter final, the *Standard*'s GAA reporter started to get excited. "Unpredictable Monaghan!" he exclaimed, in an unusually short intro. It was certainly a major upset, and judging by the accompany-ing photographs, one can only guess that the Tyrone forwards were put off their shooting by the Jimi Hendrix-style Afro on the head of Monaghan goalkeeper Kevin "Bubbles" McNeill. Two weeks later, the fever outbreak was in full spate. Monaghan trounced Cavan to reach the McKenna Cup decider for the first time since 1952, and sudden-ly, ambition was outgrowing Ulster's secondary competition. The talk now was of the Championship.

The McKenna Cup final was set for the last Sunday in May. But events in the real world intervened. The Ulster Workers' strike, of which the Dublin and Monaghan bombs were a grisly companion, had by then strangled the Six Counties. Football was a pale thing by comparison with what was happening in the news pages. And instead of a match report, the *Northern Standard* carried a mere footnote on the back of the 31 May issue, noting that the final had been called off "because of the petrol shortage and the chaotic situation in the North of Ireland". Life carried on, and football resumed in June, with Derry again the focus. This time it *was* the Ulster Championship, but Monaghan's involvement did not last long. A point down late in the game at Ballinascreen, they threw everyone forward in search of an equaliser, whereupon Derry broke away for what the *Standard* called "two stolen goals". To lose by one stolen goal might be considered unfortunate; two is stretching it. Either way, the breakthrough of Monaghan football had been postponed again. It's neither here nor there, but the number one pop record during the fever outbreak had been "Seasons in the Sun". It was succeeded in the top spot by "Waterloo". No doubt Abba's Eurovision winner sold particularly well in Monaghan.

In a year bent out of shape, the deferred McKenna Cup final was played in September, by which time the Dubs were en route to glory at Croke Park. Still, for an impoverished county, the province's secondary competition was worth winning, even if the cup would not be filled on this occasion with the promise of greater things in the summer ahead. And Monaghan's star midfielder of the time, Paddy Kerr, would later recall the defeat (for a defeat it was) as one of the most heartbreaking of his career. Kerr had won an All-Ireland club championship earlier that year with UCD, but struggled to convince his Monaghan team-mates that they were as good as most of the stars he rubbed shoulders with in Dublin. Maybe the message got through eventually, because success would soon come. A spate of McKenna Cups from 1976 onwards, a first Ulster title for forty years in 1979, and finally the glory days of the mid-1980s, in the twilight of Kerr's playing career.

But it would not come in 1974. The game was played in Monaghan town, and in a twist that only a scriptwriter who'd run out of ideas would dream of using, Derry stole another two late goals to win. This was even more poignant, because Monaghan played them off the pitch for most of the game, leading by nine points at half-time, and by a still-comfortable five as the final whistle approached. A first trophy in two decades was all but won. There were premature celebrations on the sideline. So foregone seemed the conclusion that some home supporters left early to avoid the traffic and an imminent heavy shower. Unforgivably, in a county with a substantial poultry industry, people had counted their chickens too soon. A clearly heartbroken *Northern Standard* reporter wrote of those faithful departed: "In the pubs and shops down town, they spread the good news." Back in Gavan Duffy Park, meanwhile, the wheels were coming off.

In these days of thirteen-man defences, it's hard to credit the naivety of football 1974-style. It might be helpful to recall that, in those innocent times, Monaghan's leading country and western group was still known as "The Mainliners". Anyway, such was the exuberance of the home team's play that when Derry broke up-field late in the game, most of Monaghan's defence seemed to be in the wrong half of the pitch. Veteran star Sean O'Connell, a second-half substitute, cut through what little resistance there was, passed to Frankie O'Loane, and Derry had one of the goals they needed. A minute later they had the other, again by O'Loane.

Later, in the post-match recriminations, there was criticism of the decision to bring the Monaghan team out on the pitch too soon before the game, exposing them to another of that summer's heavy showers, while Derry stayed dry in the dressing room. Perhaps the wetting explained Monaghan's late collapse. Maybe the team shrank. Whatever the reasons, when the whistle blew soon after Derry's winning goal, the *Standard* reported the Monaghan players "almost in tears". The "almost" may have been designed to spare the blushes of hard men; and sport is not worth crying over, in any case, as this book reminds us. But it was just as well for those hiding tears after the match at Gavan Duffy Park in September 1974 that, in a long wet summer, it was raining yet again.

CALL ME THE BREEZE

PAT MCCABE

I NODDED AND folded my arms, running my eyes across the roofs of the town. The shopping centre had finally been built—a brightly coloured American-style mall complete with all the high-street franchises—including the long-desired McDonald's hamburger restaurant. Austie's had been sold and was now a wine and cocktail bar—Doc Oc's—themed inside with a waterfall and exotic greenery and easy-listening music playing all day long. There were hanging flower baskets everywhere and a swanky Italian restaurant where the chip shop used to be. Stretched across the main street was a white banner with the name of his festival printed in red: "Scotsfield Breakaway Bonanza—*cominatcha*!"

We got talking some more then, and when I began to elaborate on my experiences in the entertainment field in Mountjoy, he was all ears, he really was. For that was one thing you were able to say about Connolly: he always saw the best in everyone. And if you had something to offer the parish, then he would be the man to spot it. "So you produced a concert in there, did you, Joseph?" he says, and I nodded.

"Yes," I replied, "I was very involved in all that area."

"It doesn't come as any surprise to me," he said. "I'll bet you didn't know that years ago—God bless us it must have been 1949 or '50—we did a production of *The Desert Song* with both your father and mother in it. I'll bet you didn't know that, Joseph?"

I shook my head. "No, I didn't," I said. It took me completely by surprise.

"It was absolutely terrific. Of course, your father Jamesy was a marvelous singer. There was no one to touch him in those days, Joseph. Ah yes, they were great days. You couldn't move up the street the first night it opened, that show. Another great favourite of his was 'Harbour Lights' by Jimmy Kennedy. But you'd hardly remember that. So you got on well above in Mountjoy then, did you, Joseph?"

"I was in charge of the prison garden too," I told him.

"Well, that is just fantastic," he said. "I'm glad you were able to find something that you liked, for the time would hang heavy on you now, I'm sure, if you didn't. And what else did you do?"

I told him about the concerts and my acting stint as Guard Mullaney.

"Boys," he said, "but that must have been funny. You as a policeman—I just can't picture it, Joseph!"

"Anything is possible," I found myself saying then, echoing the governor's words with a great big grin plastered across my face.

He shook his head and said: "That's the attitude! If only we had more of that attitude in Scotsfield! But, you know something, Joseph? I think it's coming!"

Extract from *Call Me the Breeze* (Faber and Faber, 2003).

MONAGHAN'S BLACK FRIDAY—
17 MAY 1974

PHILOMENA McKENNA

THE DAY STARTED with the usual trip to the post office for pensions and then the weekly shopping. The six o'clock news brought disastrous news: bombs had exploded in Dublin. Panic set in as parents wondered about their children: would they have gone from work and away from the area or were they still trapped in the aftermath? Little one thought that within the hour tragedy would have come to our own hometown.

The annual parish retreat was on, and the tea was a hurrying to get on our way to the cathedral when the silence was shattered by a mighty bang; and naturally one rushed to the front door, to be met with glass from the next house window and to see a cloud of black smoke rising from the centre of the town and the windows in the Exchange showering down on the telephonists. By this time the reality of a bomb explosion was clear to recognise, and panic broke out as it was known that three bombs had gone off in Dublin. The same pattern was expected here, with Dublin Street and Park Street being the most named areas. The local GPs and clergy and emergency services were in attendance within minutes, and the ambulance crew acted like clockwork to ferry the injured to the hospital, where staff were on full alert. Off-duty staff didn't wait to don uniforms; they just appeared from all corners.

As time slipped on, the full impact of the tragedy was emerging; and I remember Fr McSorley coming up the street, and his face showed disbelief and shock. When asked if there were any deaths, he just nodded and said, "Yes," as he hurried to the hospital.

The street was cordoned off as we waited in silence to hear if we knew any of the victims, and sadly, as the names filtered through each was recognised, as parents and families were local.

As night drew in, more streets were cordoned off, with gardaí at every entrance. The army bomb experts were examining the area and then the County Council workmen appeared, to erect barriers and to try removing some of the debris on the side streets as windows and slates were still falling. To make the task more difficult, the rain came thundering down.

The telephonists had to abandon the building; and I remember one girl coming up with blood on her hands, and on offering to take her in her response was, "Let me out of this street."

Work continued all through the night, and all one could do was keep the kettle boiling and provide warm tea to the people on duty.

Daylight on Saturday revealed the full impact of the devastation and, sadly, the confirmation of the dead. Each name meant another local family shattered. The phone lines were disrupted, and people were lined up at the phone boxes in the post office to try and get a call to relations in Dublin to check their safety and to family members elsewhere. The structural damage was so evident it was nerve-racking to look around, and as time wore on more damage came to light.

The following week the funeral processions left the hospital; and each one renewed the full tragedy as people stood in silence and tears were shed. The unspoken words in everyone's mind were, "If it had happened an hour later when the Dublin-Donegal buses had been parking for their tea break with the weekend passengers, what would have been the scale of the tragedy?"

The older residents of the town look with sadness at the spot where so many workers enjoyed their lunch in the little café, and where Greacen's was the favourite stop for the workman's evening tipple, as they offer up a silent prayer for the deceased and those who were left to mourn.

Philomena McKenna is a Mill Street resident.

APOCALYPSE

That time when Christ was circumcised
And Roman power recognised
Men made slaves of one another
Of those unlike in creed and colour.
Everything changes, nothing changes
While God's asleep the Devil ranges.

At every circus through the Empire
Loud roared the louts for blood and fire
The torching scene that got them high
Was watching others scream and die.
Everything changes, nothing changes
While God's asleep the Devil ranges.

The Prophet marched with Allah's sword
To multiply His holy word
Twin towers of death to crush us all
Pigging in squalor since the Fall.
Everything changes, nothing changes
While God's asleep the Devil ranges.

And those good crusading Christians
With their crazy inquisitions?
Sham mitres with a guilty cup
Embroidered frocks and cover up.
Everything changes, nothing changes
While God's asleep the Devil ranges.

Old bible truths all myth and honey
Are mostly about class and money
Obsessed with race and war intent
Mein Kampf a sick equivalent.
Everything changes, nothing changes
While God's asleep the Devil ranges.

The toothless bulldog of the west
Goes bellycrawling at his best
Fawning and licking Goliath's hand
Ears cocked to hear the next command.
Everything changes, nothing changes
While God's asleep the Devil ranges.

Now who can say what's false or loyal?.
While eagles eye the precious oil
The braying of a Texan ass
May trigger our apocalypse.
Everything changes, nothing changes
While God's asleep the Devil ranges.

Eugene McCabe
This was written as a protest against the war in Iraq.

Remembering

Peter Hughes

I WAS SEATED at the big front room table, making a start on my weekend homework, when the detonation noise crept in around us and pushed out the early evening calm. I remember it as a low brattle, continuing disconcertingly longer than thunder.

My grandmother, in whose Belgium Park house we lived, was a chatty countrywoman, fond of storytelling and rural lore. She had often told me of houses which had been visited by the Three Knocks, when an uncanny hand would fall three times on a door or window in a supernatural herald of death or calamity. This was supposed to "follow" certain families, she said.

The unnatural silence commanded among my mother, grandmother and me in the immediate aftermath of hearing the bomb go off was, I imagine, that induced in the recipients of such a warning. Watching the Northern Ireland news would have endowed the awful noise with an underlying familiarity for us, and contemplation of what it meant produced a dread that smothered immediate reaction.

No one started up, or shouted, "What was that?" Instead, we murmured in low, concurring voices our suspicion of what had happened, and then moved, tentatively, to the front curtains to peer out for evidence of confirmation, a pattern probably repeated in every one of the bungalows in our row and in houses throughout the Belgium Park estate, located a brisk five-minute walk from where the bomb went off.

Very few of the Park people had telephones. Front gates became points of exchange for information, huddles where two, three or four neighbours would weigh each other's news, sifting through the early rumour and speculation, retaining the hard nuggets of fact that began to flow up from the town and circulating these among themselves. It soon emerged that the sound of the bomb going off had indeed been a portent of death and injury, passing our own house by but touching others very close to us.

It was strange to watch Monaghan on the news as the evening and weekend unfolded, described with the same lexicon of devastation the newscasters customarily used for Belfast, adjuncted to the kin, unfolding horror stories of the Dublin bombs. Footage of the bomb scene showed a familiar part of the town, garbled and distorted in nightmare fashion. For me, the stern maternal admonition, "Don't you be going down that town!" was unnecessary. I had no immediate wish to see this any closer.

When I did, going to school on the Monday, it was the laying waste of Jack McGlone's café that tore at me the sharpest. Of all the tumbled buildings and structures, this seemed most a landmark to me, a treat-time stopping off point during rounds of the shops throughout my childhood. Jack McGlone's had been possessed in my mind of folkloric immutability, had its own place in Monaghan parlance: the joke rendezvous "Upstairs in Jack McGlone's" a cliché of cornerboy wit. Jack McGlone was my neighbour, the genial, soccer-crazy man at the end of my row, who never tired of watching our kickabouts on the Green and who was now fighting for his life in hospital.

I saw the bursted-apart timber of the café, its cheery colours heartbreaking now, and the rubble and ruin of the buildings around it from the window of my school bus, and from this vantage point watched Church Square's slow mending, as the days and weeks passed by.

After a time my friend and neighbour Alan, whose mother Peggy was killed in the bomb, came back to school, and often we would sit together on the bus.

In the vicinity of his deep, self-contained sadness, I felt I was no good to him. Because my father had died when I was six years old, I suppose I thought I ought to be. But in the silences between us on those bus journeys, there began for me, at the cusp of adolescence, the learning of a lesson that has received intermittent revision over the course of my life to date: that experience of personal loss doesn't equip you any way better to provide insightful comfort to others similarly bereaved. My way of dealing with my father's death was adherence to what seemed then a useful trait: I kept that sort of thing to myself. I sat beside Alan on the bus and hoped that he would do the same, and it is my recollection that mostly he did.

Time passed, and I continued to watch the superficial healing of the town from the school bus window. Jack McGlone recovered health sufficient to allow him resume watching our scurrying football games on the Green. In time, mirroring its founder, McGlone's café came back heroically, too.

At some point in the intervening years, my eldest brother Johnny told me that he should have been walking past Greacen's pub on his way to our house in Belgium Park when the bomb went off. It was his habit on Friday evenings after work, before going home to the Mall Road, to call up to the home place in the Park for his tea. He always came bearing a trove of comics for me, but the visit was postponed this Friday evening because he was working late. But unknown to me for long time, Johnny got finished a bit earlier than expected and changed his plans. He was just getting ready to leave the *Northern Standard* office and head to Belgium Park, intending to go round by Greacen's to get to Hamill's newsagents for my comics, when the bomb exploded. When I'm reminded of the Monaghan bomb now, the first thing that slips into my mind is my brother's description of its noise, and the sound like torrential rain that followed as debris fell on the galvanised roof of the printing house where he worked. And I am always thankful that other, more clement forces at work that night held him for precious minutes within the eye of that storm.

MEMORY

TONY SWIFT

MY NAME IS Tony Swift, from Belgium Park, Monaghan. I am a retired sub-station officer with Monaghan Fire Service, which in 1974 was a part-time service. I will always remember clearly the events of that terrible day. I was just after finishing work in a local dry cleaners in Park Street, and I had arranged to meet my brother-in-law, Myles Eardley, in the Westenra Hotel. At that time my means of transport was a bicycle, which we needed to respond to fire calls quickly. I passed Greacen's and was in the Westenra just a few minutes when the building rocked with a loud explosion. My first thought was that a fuel tank in the hotel yard had exploded, so I ran out to check. When I saw that the tank was intact, I went out to the street in front of the hotel which is called the Diamond. I felt a weird silence and saw shattered glass all around. It was then that I thought that maybe this was a bomb.

The fire siren was set off at that minute; this was our call-out means, as there was no bleeper system at that time. The siren sounded three times for a normal call-out, but if it went off for longer, that meant that the situation was serious and we would need the assistance of the Auxiliary Fire Service, Civil Defence. Well, the siren kept going, so I knew it was a bomb.

When we arrived at the scene there was total mayhem. Jack McGlone's café was engulfed in flames, and there were cars burning close by. The café was totally destroyed, as was Greacen's pub. We entered the building in search of casualties. I can still recall the casualties being carried to waiting ambulances; everybody that was in the area was trying to help others. The emergency services and the local people were a credit.

That night and the next day there was a general clean-up of the streets and inspection of damaged buildings. To the day I die I will never forget that evening and the shock, the numbness and sadness of the Monaghan people at the events which destroyed their friends and the town.

SKIN OF DREAMS

EVELYN CONLON

DURING THE WEEKS after the death of P. Joe and Cassie Mannering, time slowed almost to a standstill for Maud. There was an acuteness about each minute. She went back to work, exhausted from all the talking to people, almost looking forward to a desk, office correspondence, an excuse not to dive into answers to platitudinous questions. But there were times when she seemed to go rigid with fear. The feeling might start in her hand or her ribs or her elbow; no matter where, it fanned itself out until her whole body was stiff as a frozen stick. Minutes were like a house of cards: one of them fell, and the game of getting through the next hour collapsed. She felt cold. Everything was new. *This is the first time I have taken an appointment since. . . . This is the first time I have had a tuna sandwich since. . . . This is the first time I have watched the nine o'clock news since. . . .* She heard references to things that had happened a week ago, but they were lost to her, they had never occurred.

The first time she went to the butcher shop, she said, "A pork chop, please." She lifted a dozen free range eggs from the side of the counter and placed them in front of her. The butcher looked at her quizzically as he put the chops beside the eggs. He shivered.

"Someone has just walked over my grave," he said, then laughed nervously.

Maud was terrified. She stammered, "How much is that?"

She hurried from the shop. She felt that she should go back to tell him. Otherwise he would not know what had caused that ripple of cold. He might worry this evening. He might have a nightmare tonight. She did not go back. It was better that some people didn't know what terrible thing had happened to her. But it distressed her to know that her grief was such a living thing that it walked with her and created a disturbance for strangers.

"It will take time," people said, and she wondered what they knew about time.

"Are your parents alive?" she asked.

If only it had been just one of them. She liked people best if they had a mother or father dead. She preferred those who had no parents alive. Both bookends gone.

Malachy stayed home most evenings, although he would have preferred to busy himself away from their flat. They drank too much. Maud opened bottles of wine and marvelled at the greatness of drink, how the first glass vanished pain like a magician might. Towards the end of the third glass the magic wavered, and something like disappointment or a merciless sorrow crowded over them. They needed each other desperately, one to talk, one to listen, to disagree about the sequence of things that had happened, to help each other put order on their pasts, which had become living things and much longer than their actual years. They both knew that this swimming in agony would have to stop, that they could not put their feet up to doom, as if it was a warm fire, but they were reluctant to leave unsaid the things that needed airing and even more loth to take the blind leap into the parentless future. Valerie felt left out, but her workmates advised her to leave them be for a while. It would be better in the long run to let them weep in private. But despite this advice, she worried that one of them would get over the immediate pain quicker than the other; her suspicions about which one it would be changed daily.

The three of them went to the month's mind mass together. As the priest flourished his way through the comforting familiarities, Maud suppressed the memories that were too hard to bear. She dreaded the handshakes with neighbours that were now bound to happen and removed the ring from her right hand so that it did not become sore, as it had at the funeral. But she was surprised to discover how the neighbours' genuine concern made her feel fine, or at least finer. They went to the local pub afterwards, where their parents had had their quiet few drinks every Saturday night, always going home before closing time, an unnatural thing in itself.

Valerie said, "I'll do the driving back to Dublin so that the two of you can have a few drinks with everyone. There's no need for all of us to stay sober."

It was the kindest of offers. On the way to the pub they passed their old house. Maud and Malachy turned together to stare at it. As

Valerie drove on, they turned their heads and even looked out the back window. Valerie slowed down.

"Would either of you like to go in?" she asked.

Maud said, "No, not yet. Next week, Saturday, if that's all right with you, both of you."

Valerie had obviously been asked to join them. The house would have to be cleaned up. There was no way out of that. So Saturday it was.

* * *

The house had originally been a cottage, a square cottage, but it had finicky additions, including a half-upstairs, which gave it a body and a face. The roof was crooked in places, and the garden was full. The bushes came right up to the side walls. The assortment of flowers was in almost continuous bloom, decay, bloom. It had always been kept tidy and clean, but not overfussy. As they neared it on that Saturday, Malachy speeded up as if to avoid watching its approach. When Maud got out of the car, she went towards the front door, head bowed, key ready in her hand. She could have sworn there was a washing on the line, flapping, slapping, but that wasn't possible. It was a hard journey from the gate to the door. Malachy stood back and let Maud turn the key. She pushed the door against some letters. Who could possibly have sent letters? Who could possibly not have known? The names on them were too unbearable to be taken seriously.

Maud thought that there were two kinds of mothers, those who could watch their children having injections and those who shiver uncontrollably as they try to lie to their child that it won't hurt. The latter are in serious trouble. Theirs was like that, constantly in love, saying sorry to her children. Malachy heard their mother talking loudly about them when they were teenagers, covering worry. A neighbour had visited once with her young baby. Their mother had put the child on the sofa and said, "Look at you, sitting up there with your great little straight back, and you not six months. You're a genius." She had been like that, giving generous credit where it was not necessarily due.

In the dead quiet of the house, nothing was breathing except the fridge. They had forgotten to switch it off, on the forlorn evening that they had left it. The street outside was empty of teenagers, and because it was a wet windy day, no mothers were taking small children out for a breath. But you could feel them behind the curtains, waiting for a respectable time to pass before they would call to see if anything needed doing. When they had made a cup of tea—Valerie had remembered to bring teabags, milk, scones and butter—real sounds came back into the room. There was an audible shuffle of feet; it could have belonged to the doctors coming down the hospitable corridor to talk to Malachy and Maud on that evening. There had been two of them, one each. Or they could have belonged to the dead and their living children.

"Jesus Christ, the goldfish. We forgot about the goldfish," Maud said, putting her hand over her mouth. All three of them laughed nervously.

"Will we bury them or what?"

Maud remembered them circling the bowl and taking sporadic darts towards each other as if to kiss. It became very important to get them out of the house. Malachy said that he would do it, and when he came back in, the women didn't ask him where nor how. They felt mean for not having offered to go to the garden with him.

"Right then, we'll take a room each," said Malachy, the schoolteacher. Valerie was certainly one of them now. "Stack similar things together. We'll get proper packers in for what we want to keep. Put all the clothes together."

It sounded easy. And despite the occasional strangled cry, it became just a day's work, with breaks for food from the nearby takeaway. Two neighbours did call briefly, but knew to leave them to it, and spread the word to the others.

"We'll be having a drink later, at ten, say. Down in the hotel bar."

And when ten o'clock came, it was all, "What are you having?"

The drinks gave them the courage to stay in the house that night, Maud in her old room, Malachy and Valerie in his.

"I'll start on the boxes in the attic in the morning," Maud said, as if the job would be an ordinary task.

It is presumed, indeed wished, that a person will find at least bones in a dead parent's cupboard. Maud had two parents dead at the same time, not giving one of them a chance to censor, so she knew that she would find some unexplained things in the attic. It was a useful thought. It helped her flick through the paper paraphernalia of a life, two lives. When she found the packet, sternly overwrapped, with layers of paper and sellotape, she knew that this was it. But she had expected maybe love letters from unknown people or a child thing, a birth thing—that was always the big one. This was what she found.

Dear Brigid,

I write this letter with a heavy heart but with some glimmer of consolation, even if it is one that cannot rectify the injustice done. Your brother sent for me last Tuesday evening, and, as I drove over to see him, I was in quite a rage thinking, now he will tell me that he did do it. I tell you this only so you will know that I was not automatically predisposed to believing him. But when I was shown in to see him, I knew by his countenance that I had been wrong to have doubts. He told me that he had been thinking of my possible doubts and that he wanted to reassure me. He had not murdered Moll Graney. He could not, would not, murder anybody, and certainly not his defenseless neighbour whom he had rather pitied, yet admired. But he told me that I was not to carry this with me for the rest of my life, that I had done all that was humanly possibly. He said that there was no point now in going over the details of his defence. He said that he was ready to meet his God and that I could go now. We shook hands. I have never experienced such a handshake.

When I reached the door, he said that if, in time, I felt there was anything I could do, he would appreciate it if I could help to clear his name. It wouldn't matter one whit to him, he said, but it might, to you and children to come. He was serene. He smiled at me. On my way out the governor shuffled more than normal, and told me that he thought that an innocent man was going to be hanged.

I prayed very hard on Wednesday morning, as I am sure you did. I will be in touch soon. Rest assured that I will not let this story rest.

Yours sincerely,
Sean MacBride.

The parcel also included newspaper clippings, further letters from the barrister, a neck tie, a music book, a book on greyhounds and a photograph of a tall man holding a small child.

Maud drew in deep breaths of disbelief. This had to be her mother's uncle. Her mother had had an uncle, one other than Hugh. Her mother had had an uncle, and he had murdered a woman and had been hanged for it. But according to this letter, he had not murdered a woman and had been hanged for it. Her mother had never told them. Her mother's Uncle Hugh had never told them. This man had not just been hanged for something he didn't do; he had been so efficiently airbrushed out of existence he might never have been born.

And the neighbours would have known. All their lives, the neighbours would have known. All their bloody lives, their mother, their mother's uncle, their father, she presumed, had known. Had the neighbours' children known? The people who went to school with them? The people on the school bus? The bus driver with the twinkling eyes and the exciting smell of drink? Their teachers, oh God, their teachers, her first teacher who always told her that she was good at school and would make a teacher herself, the shopkeeper in the shop where they bought sweets? The big fat shopkeeper with the chins rolling down into each other? Had they all known? And had they wondered if she and Malachy knew?

Oh my good God.

Maud sat for a while rereading, unwilling to move from the quiet and must of the room. Although in normal circumstances she would have immediately discussed a matter as important as this, indeed as shattering as this, with Malachy, she put the parcel aside and decided to wait until she had digested the enormity of the discovery before talking to him. It would be best if at least one of them could allow reactions to settle before discussing it. She did not admit that she was a little afraid of how Malachy might react, nor that she had a strong niggling desire not to let Valerie know. Already, having known this thing a mere few minutes, she was doing exactly as her mother had done. The thumping of a person with a secret has effect. Even the act of returning the knowledge to secrecy produces effect. She thought about this as her heart picked up speed, missing some beats and creating a feeling of air in her head. She could hear noises from downstairs, the clanking of pots, pans, crockery, kitchen accessories being arranged together. What would they do with it all?

Rain began to fall, then intensify, becoming the only outside noise. She went downstairs, remarkably steadily, she thought, having picked up a box of photographs which would do to break the ice.

"Remember this," she said, and Malachy and Valerie stood one at each of her shoulders looking at the picture, their physical closeness like a blanket being put over a wet cold body. "This is at Portrush. Our aunt took it, our father's sister, during the war. The telegraph poles were hammered down into the beach so that enemy planes couldn't land. The seals came in, and as the tide was going out, one of them got caught on a pole. This woman, who swam every day, all year round, thought she would save him. She borrowed an umbrella and swam out. Everyone on the shore watched. They were delighted when she managed to poke him off the pole, but no sooner had she turned to swim back towards them than the seal was back again."

Valerie touched Maud on the shoulder. There had been a lot of that this day, touching, holding, hugging. It would have to stop sometime soon. Malachy said, "We have only one aunt on my father's side, and my mother had only one uncle."

"Yeah," said Maud.

They left the house that evening, having decided to make no decision yet about what to do with it.

Extract from *Skin of Dreams*, Brandon, 2003.

Monaghan Memory

Mary Berwick

J UST BEFORE THE bomb went off, Joe was outside talking to Archie Harper. I knocked the window to let him know his tea was ready. Leaving Mr Harper, he came into the kitchen, passing through the dining room where the three children were watching TV. As he sat down there was a loud noise, the doors flew off the cooker, fridge and presses, and part of the ceiling came down. I had been standing at the cooker, in line with the window, and with the force was blown straight out into the back kitchen. Joe was protected by the wall, and his first reaction was, "What have you done to the bank's cooker?" (I had been cooking meringues for a school cake sale, and initially he thought I was responsible!)

However, he quickly realised that it was a bomb. Our concern was for the children. There was an eerie silence, with no sound coming from the dining room. The door couldn't be opened as the carpet had lifted (the door opened inwards), but fortunately there was another door from the hall. The fear and panic were agonising as we saw the door blown off, but the children were sitting on the floor, covered in soot, shocked into silence, surrounded by broken glass. The large marble fireplace had fallen and was in bits, and all the soot had come down the chimney.

The heavy wooden pelmet extending over two windows and measuring 10 feet had crashed down on the couch where the children had been sitting, but luckily they had been thrown to the floor. The TV landed upside down in the opposite corner of the room, and to this day still works perfectly, although badly pitted with glass.

The plate glass from the windows, 1 centimetre thick, was lodged like shelves into the opposite wall. Miraculously, the children were unharmed, the only damage being that Karen's hair was shaved by flying glass. Once we realised that the children were safe, nothing else mattered.

A few minutes later a sound registered—it was the song

"Somewhere over the Rainbow" being played on an old 78 record. On the top landing was an old-fashioned gramophone, the arm of which had dropped down on the record, and the music seemed like a shocking intrusion.

Joe sent our son Adrian, then eleven years, out to bring Mr Harper into the house, but sadly the poor man was critically injured. I ran across to Greacen's pub, and the sight was horrific. By this time people were arriving on the scene, and one of our staff, Peter McLaughlin, kindly took our children up to friends. A man asked me for sheets or blankets, and I raced upstairs to the hot press. In the bank there was a spiral staircase, and I had to scramble over a grandmother clock that had come down the stairs and was lodged there.

The gardaí and emergency services came quickly and were very efficient in setting up barricades and taping off the area. Two gardaí came into the bank and asked to go into the office. Joe said, "Certainly, wait till I get the keys," and didn't understand why the gardaí looked at him peculiarly. There was no door left into the office!

One of the strange things that occurred was that things which were inside the house flew out of the doors and windows and things that were outside came in. In the drawing room upstairs were parts of the car that held the bomb, but hanging from the spouting was my daughter's dressing gown, which had been in the kitchen.

At this stage the gardaí rushed in and told us there was a bomb in the Courthouse and to run down by Swan Lake. We were halfway down when a squad car came in the opposite direction and told us to go back, that there was another bomb down there. Fortunately they were hoaxes.

We went back to the bank and started the business of barricading the premises. However, top of the list was getting word to our families who all lived in Dublin. A friend offered to go to Castleblayney to try to ring from there. Unfortunately my mother was visiting friends and couldn't be contacted and saw the nine o'clock news. She got such a shock, especially when she saw the bank and learned that five people had been killed. She assumed it was us and collapsed with the shock. Actually she never really recovered fully and had to sell up and come to live with us. (By that time we were in a rented house.)

On a lighter note, our dog suffered shell-shock and totally refused to go into the bank after that night. He became very protective of the children and would allow nobody near them.

We stayed in the Four Seasons Hotel for a few nights after the bomb, and rather than risk a refusal, we sneaked the dog in every night. Joe would pass him in through the window. However, with people walking up and down the corridor late at night and early in the morning, I had to sit with my hand over his mouth in case he barked and gave the show away.

Death and Nightingales

Eugene McCabe

O N THE SECOND floor of Enniskillen Town Hall Mr Gary Pringle could see, through a gap in the high door, the low platform where Miss Sarah Egerton, organist at St Anne's Church of Ireland, had been playing melodies now for almost half an hour, all of them associated with Mr Percy French. Having exhausted these she was now moving uncertainly to other popular pieces. She sat at an upright piano placed sideways to the audience. To the right of this piano there was a podium ready for Mr French, on which were placed a paraffin lamp, a glass and a decanter full of water. The large reception chamber was full. It was warm, and an usher was trying to open the high, broad windows with a long pole.

The committee members in the lobby downstairs were becoming anxious. Two of them had been to the railway station. Mr French was expected on the six-thirty which he should have caught at Clones junction. He was not on that. They surmised he must be arriving by gig. This information was relayed to Mr Pringle upstairs, who could now see the Protestant Bishop of Clogher looking at his pocket-watch. Aware that Miss Egerton was moving to the concluding chords of "Carrickfergus", he cleaned his spectacles, adjusted his bow-tie and walked through the high door onto the low platform. Acting-cashier with the Bank of Ireland on the main street, a producer and performer in amateur musicals, he was widely regarded in town and county as something of a wag and raconteur. Standing beside the podium he begged for silence with open hands:

"What we hear about Mr Percy French is that he can be somewhat late but never disappoints. At the moment he is somewhat late. Can we in the meantime not entertain ourselves? I see both Bishops of Clogher here. One is a renowned traveller, a builder of cathedrals and to my certain knowledge has a fine singing voice."

There was much looking around, until William Armstrong, the Protestant Bishop of Clogher, said in clear tones from the second row:

"*That* is most certainly *not me*."

He had a cold, white face, almond eyes, and kept his mouth fixed in a kind of smile. Attention now moved from the second row to somewhere near the back where James Donnelly, the Catholic Bishop of Clougher, was heard to mutter:

"My God, what a gaffe!" He was seated between his sister and his Curate, Benny Cassidy, who now whispered:

"'You'll have to sing now or be damned; you've no choice, he'll torture you till you do."

Jimmy Donnelly stood and began walking towards the platform amidst tepid clapping from one half of the audience, warm applause from the other. The Earl of Enniskillen, blind grandmaster of the Orange Lodge, inclined his head towards his daughter and asked:

"Can you describe him, dear?"

"He's tiny, Papa, smaller than me and pert with a pursed-up mouth, white hair and sort of a mincy walk. He's got very good eyes and his suit looks a lot smarter than yours."

Through the hum of audience expectation Jimmy Donnelly was now consulting with Miss Egerton who had often seen priests in the streets of Enniskillen. Never in her life had she spoken to one. Here now, she was with a Catholic Bishop; her head averted, nodding, her lips moving. Yes she could manage that, yes she knew the song well, yes and that melody too. As her fingers automatically began to phrase a few bars, Jimmy Donnelly turned to the audience and said in a clear tenor voice which was unexpectedly rich and almost accentless:

"The reason I sing occasionally in my garden is because of necessity, when I sing in the house my dog Solomon howls and howls and howls. I think my dog has good judgement." There was a share of scattered clapping, tolerant smiling and Miss Egerton was obliged to restart the introduction to "Kathleen Mavoorneen", one of the Bishop's two party pieces, the other being "Charlie is my darling". Some said this was a cheeky tilt at his retired predecessor, Charles McNally, who once said to him coldly at a clerical dinner:

"You're not just silly, Jimmy, you're childish betimes."

Eight words which still hurt. Those more politically inclined thought it had more to do with his warm approval of the politics of Mr Charles Stewart Parnell.

From the back of the hall an usher now beckoned to Gary Pringle. He went over, listened, nodding and smiling. As he left by the side door Jimmy Donnelly was beginning the first verse of "Kathleen Mavoorneen".

It took five minutes to establish that Mr Percy French was coming up the street. By then Jimmy Donnelly was rising emotionally to the last line, his neck craned up as markedly as Miss Egerton's was bent sideways and down towards the soft pedal and the concluding chords. The audience response was genuine and warm.

Gary Pringle smiled, waiting for this to stop. Inclining his head towards Donnelly, he said: "From what I've just heard, your dog Solomon is a poor judge!"

He waited until the Bishop had retaken his seat and then said:

"I have just received the most agreeable confirmation. Mr Percy French is now in the town and is, as I speak, making his way here with all possible dispatch. He is not, may I hasten to add, as some have suggested, 'travelling with Miss Brady in her private ass and cart'."

There was some good-natured laughing.

Outside on the Diamond it was mild for early May, with happily no hint of late-spring sharpness. On account of this, a great many town and country people who could not afford tickets for the performance were waiting to see and welcome Mr French.

Billy Winters and Mickey Dolphin had just come from stabling Punch at the Royal Hotel. As they arrived to the top of the stairs leading to the Town Hall there was a mix of clapping and laughter from lower down the main street. An usher shouted from the lobby:

"He's here! He'll be up directly!" And indeed, there he was, cheerfully doffing his boater to someone waving from a window, shaking hands genially, talking and laughing with people as he moved through the crowd towards the lobby; meeting yet again what he met everywhere: the barefoot world of street and field he wrote and sang about to entertain the booted world that crowded in to hear him in halls and theatres.

After about a minute's delay he emerged from the crowd, mounting the stone steps of the Town Hall, his straw boater in one hand and the other extended towards Billy Winters. Both spoke simultaneously:

"My dear fellow."

"My dear Billy."

The embrace and handclasps were warm and mutual, but because of the press of people and officials they could not hear each other properly. Billy Winters' invitation to Clonoula could not be accepted:

"No, no, I wish I could . . ."

He glanced back at his wife. She shook her head saying:

"We're booked into Irvinestown . . . We leave straight after."

Just then Billy Winters realised that Mickey Dolphin was calling him urgently.

"Mr Billy Sorr! Mr Billy Sorr!"

Turning he saw an usher in a bow-tie gripping Mickey's arm above the elbow, escorting him towards the door.

"What in the hell are you at?" Billy called out.

"This hoeboy has no ticket," the usher said over his shoulder, "and he's drunk I'd swear."

"I'd swear he's not, and he's no 'hoeboy', he's my friend Michael Dolphin, and this," Billy said, holding up a small docket, "is his ticket."

Percy French adjusted his own bow-tie, leaned towards Billy and said in a whisper:

"One thing for sure I surely know,

Trust no man in a dickie-bow."

Aloud he said:

"If Michael Dolphin is a friend of my friend Billy Winters then he's a friend of mine."

With his arm around Mickey Dolphin's shoulder they moved as three from the lobby to the broad staircase leading to the upper hall and straight into the chamber and a tumult of exploding applause. The impression created was of a flamboyant circus performer with his arm around an Indian snake-charmer, with Billy Winters two paces behind . . . a smiling promoter.

Half-way down the aisle, Percy French found a seat for Mickey Dolphin, then paused as a young girl proffered a songbook for his signature. He stooped, bargaining for a kiss which was given before signing. All the while Miss Egerton was playing "The Darlin' Girl from Clare", addressing the chords with great feeling and flourish, and a side-to-side shaking of her head.

On the platform Mr Gary Pringle stood beside the podium waiting to introduce Percy French, who now joined him. The response was so sustained that the singer became emotional, and tried once or twice with a wave of the left hand to make it stop. When it did, Gary Pringle moved forward and said:

"It would be impertinent to introduce our guest. Only last week the London *Times* described him as a 'phenomenon', an Irishman of Planter stock equally loved by all breeds and creeds of his fellow Irishmen. Ladies and gentlemen, we are all here this evening to welcome to the town of Enniskillen, that phenomenon in person, Mr Percy French, from Frenchpark in the county of Roscommon."

During the applause the singer poured a glass of water from the decanter into the tumbler, drank a mouthful, and Welsh-combed his moustache and hair. When silence came he said, "I want to begin with a poem for a friend I haven't seen for years. He will know why."

He then spoke the words of "Gort-na-Mona" in such a natural unforced voice that people thought at first that he was making a few introductory remarks. When the poem ended he said quickly, "A sad start, you see, allows me to have a happy ending and I believe in happy endings." He winked at the audience and began telling them about the West Clare Railway and the origin of the ballad "Are you right there Michael, are you right", an account they found as hilarious as his eventual singing of the ballad itself.

He then sang "Phil the Fluther", clowning round the small stage, playing peek-a-boo with Miss Egerton, using his banjo as a gun or club, pointing and winking at dignitaries and the audience who now clapped rhythmically as Miss Egerton worked overtime with fingers and pedals and the heels of her sensible shoes. When this piece was concluded, and during the response to it, he took out a handkerchief and wiped his face. He drank more water, waiting for silence:

"Walking up your main street," he said, "'I saw legends in a few shop windows: 'Go to Canada for three pounds by Dominion Line'— and other advertisements for other companies promoting America, Australia, South Africa; shipping lines all competing to take us away from what should be paradise, and I thought: why do we always long to be elsewhere? Do we not belong here? What are we looking for? Glory or a grave? God? Cheap gin? A *New* World? For whatever reason we still leave in our thousands and thousands and this seems to me such heartbreak that I was forced to write a funny song about it."

Miss Egerton was introducing "The Mountains of Mourne" again when a young bearded man stood up in the middle of the hall. He had a folded newspaper in one hand and waved it baton-like towards the stage. Percy French motioned with one hand towards the piano. Miss Egerton stopped playing. Billy Winters, two rows from the front, looked back at the interrupter. He had a monkish face and slight figure, probably one of Parnell's Lieutenants or Davitt's cronies: an agitator, a Land Leaguer, a Fenian crackpot. He could see Mr Gary Pringle urgently beckoning ushers from the back. When the murmur of the audience stopped Percy French said quietly:

"Yes, Sir?"

The young man said in a clear voice that everyone could hear: "Your Ireland, Sir, is all fun, no funerals; all questions and no answers."

Here and there people whispered, lips moving angrily. The young man waited for them to stop. Someone from the front shouted back: "Sit down or get out!"

Realising he might be shouted down he raised his voice: "'Why do we leave,' you ask, 'what's wrong here?' you ask and 'The Mountains of Mourne' which you are about to sing is indeed a comic and affecting song, but . . .'"

From all over the hall people now began to murmur and mutter: "Idiot! Sit down! Get out! Damned Crackpot!"

Percy French with upraised hands, waited for silence. Through the interruption he had smiled. Now he said, "I'm sure you have something serious to say, Sir, but these people, God help their wit, have travelled and paid money *to hear me.*"

The hall broke out into a storm of clapping and more shouts of "Sit down," "Fenian" and "Leaguer" and "lout". When someone shouted: "To hell with Parnell," the atmosphere became suddenly unpleasant.

The interrupter stood unmoved, waiting for the noise and abuse to stop. When it did, he waved his newspaper again, "May I read one small item from your *Impartial Reporter*, published today Thursday, 3rd May, 1883?"

There were more shouts of "come on" and "we can read for our-selves".

"Is it a long item?" Percy French asked.

"It's very short," the young man said.

"Let's hear it then."

The young man opened the newspaper and began:

"The heading says: 'Distress in Glencolumbkille'. A sub-heading: 'Potatoes and meal exhausted'."

He had to wait through a hubbub of objections before he could continue:

"'Extraordinary scenes greeted our Majesty's government inspector Dr Woodhouse in the village of Glencolumbkille last weekend. Dr Woodhouse was besieged on arrival by 2,000 semi-starving people; men, women and children begging, kneeling, crying out. Visibly affected he could not make himself heard above the wailing until the Reverend Thomas Gallagher arrived to restore order.'"

The two ushers were now moving from the side aisles towards where he stood. Seeing them approach, the young man said:

"Clearly, Sir, I'm not going to be permitted to read on."

"It looks a bit like that," Percy French said.

"Then may I say that your comic song about exile makes me unwell every time I hear it."

From the back of the hall a voice shouted:

"Blackguard!" followed by more shouts of "Fenian!", "Villain!" and "Murderer!"

A young woman began to clap and shout support for the young man as he was led out. She was joined by other voices until gradually the audience became a cacophony of howling, shouting and clapping.

When the interrupter was gone Percy French waited for silence, looking very closely at the nails on his right hand and then on his left and all the time smiling to himself. When he said, "Well!" there was an uneasy response. When he said, "Well and apparently unwell," the uneasy response became uneasy laughter. He waited for it to fade:

"If you happen to ask what's wrong in this country," he began, "the knife-grinders go to work. Yes, Glencolumbkille is terrible, and so is Calcutta and the Gorbals and all the poor ends of a thousand cities the world over. Today, yesterday, tomorrow, it's all heartbreaking, and all of us who live on this little island and love it probably imagine we know it well till some fine morning or evening like this, we discover suddenly that we're strangers in a strange place, where terrible things happen and you feel maybe the ship is going down. Now if you know the ship is sinking you can bail out till it goes down or you can sing funny songs. I favour the latter course. A high-falutin' 'gent' in the *Irish Times* once described what I do as 'a type of bucolic burlesque'; I wasn't sure if I was being commended or condemned so I went to the dictionary. It means country fun of a low kind, the opposite it would seem to city fun of a high kind. The last time I was in the Rotunda Theatre a young lad in pantaloons was singing his heart out for a lady who must have weighed in at around twenty stones. May God preserve me from such weighty works of art."

Billy Winters listened fascinated as his old college comrade winked, grinned, and with gentle mockery and self-mockery, talked, clowned, sang and recited his way back into the heart of the audience. Gradually the darkness of anger was replaced by the brightness of comedy. When he ended very deliberately with "The Mountains of Mourne" the entire hall erupted into a cheering pandemonium. It went on and on, with shouts of, "More, more, more;" so much so that he was forced to take out a pocket-watch. He dangled it with one hand pointing at the face with his left forefinger then pointing off-stage to indicate that he had to go. Finally he left, waving, smiling like a child at an elated, enraptured, cheering audience. Minutes later his trap was at the front of the Town Hall, his wife standing on the pavement holding the door open.

Half-way to the hollow of the town, as he returned greetings from window and street, from public house and private doorway, he could still hear Miss Egerton on the piano as she accompanied most of the audience singing in loyal chorus: "God Save the Queen".

Extract from *Death and Nightingales*
(Secker & Warburg, 1992).

NOTE

(for Jacqueline Bardwell)

The trouble is I miss the short sea
in an alcove of rock or the wider
more impelling stretch of the Atlantic
I seem to be paralysed between two Drumlins
and the trees against the pewter clouds
unnerve me as though to say "I know your number".

Still at the moment, all is well
and when the time is right
I shall go—there are other places
somewhere with a Russian wind talking down the
    chimney
and the Black Sea breaking wilfully
beyond the reaches of Chekov's garden.

Leland Bardwell

BIOGRAPHIES

Leland Bardwell. Born in India. Poet, short-story writer, playwright and novelist. Lived in Monaghan for many years and is trustee of the Katherine Kavanagh estate. She now lives in Sligo.

Evelyn Conlon. Born 1952 in Rockcorry. Educated Coravaccan NS, St Louis' Convent, Monaghan, NUI Maynooth. Author of three collections of short stories and three novels, she has edited two other anthologies. She lives in Dublin.

Patrick Duffy. Born in Cremartin. Associate professor of geography at NUI Maynooth, teaching historical, rural and landscape studies. Author of *Landscapes of South Ulster*, 1993.

Peter Hughes. Native of Monaghan town. Senior journalist with the *Northern Standard*. A published poet, he was shortlisted for a Hennessy Award in 1998.

John McArdle. A native of Drumhowan. Actor, director, teacher, dramatist, he has written plays for all ages. He won a Hennessy Award for short stories and wrote for *Glenroe* for five years.

Eugene McCabe. Born in Glasgow in 1930, he has lived and farmed at Drumard, Clones, for the last fifty years. He has written plays for stage and television, has published short stories, novels and occasional verse.

Pat McCabe. Born in Clones, 1955. Novelist, playwright and children's short-story writer, he has been shortlisted for the Booker Prize. He now lives in Clones.

Nell McCafferty. Born in the Bogside, Derry, in 1944. Her life story, *Nell*, covering civil rights in the North and feminism in the South, will be published worldwide by Penguin in October 2004.

Ted McCarthy. Born 1957 in Clones, educated St Tiernach's and St Pat's, Drumcondra, he has taught in County Monaghan since graduation. Widely published in anthologies throughout the world.

Paddy MacEntee. Born in Monaghan 1936, educated St Louis', Christian Brothers' and St Macartan's, UCD and King's Inns. Called to the Bar 1960. Senior counsel 1975, Bar of Northern Ireland and QC. Practises as a barrister specialising in criminal law.

Frank McNally. Born in Carrickmacross, educated at Patrician Brothers' High School. Reporter and columnist for *The Irish Times*.

Shane Martin. Born in Carrickmacross. Is widely published in anthologies and has two collections of poetry. He lives in Monaghan.

Hugh Maxton. Poet, translator, academic. Professor of literary history at Goldsmith College, London. He now lives in Rockcorry.

Ciarán Ó Cearnaigh. Born in Dublin, 1970. Educated at NCAD. Works primarily in video and film. Has exhibited widely in both group and solo shows.

Mary O'Donnell. Educated at St Louis', Monaghan, and later at NUI Maynooth. She is a novelist, short-story writer and poet.

Aidan Rooney-Céspedes. Born in Monaghan in 1965. He has been awarded many prizes, including the Hennessy Award. He now lives and teaches in Massachusetts.

Padraig Rooney. Born in Monaghan in 1956. A novelist and poet, he has been awarded the Patrick Kavanagh Award. He now lives and teaches in Switzerland.

Peter Woods. Born in Lisdoonan and lived for many years in London and elsewhere in Europe. Novelist and radio producer for RTÉ.